Delphi's Dilemma

Book 2 in 'The Strong Sisters' series

Ros Rendle

ISBN: 978-1-78808-702-5

Cover design: Ros and Scott Rendle

Printed and bound in Great Britain by BookPrintingUK
http://www.bookprintinguk.com

Also available on Amazon:
Sense and French Ability – Ros Rendle (Endeavour Press)

Peace of Time – Ros Rendle (Endeavour Press)

Flowers of Flanders – Book 1 in 'The Strong Sisters' series

For Cathy and Libby
This is a story of a mother and her child. I'm particularly fortunate
to have two daughters.

Chapter 1

On board the SS Jervis Bay 1927

Now they had left sight of land Delphi could see how the next thirty days or so might be. Surely this was the right decision. After all these years she had been jittery about making the move but having got this far she persuaded herself it was definitely a good result. She should take ten years old Flora to meet her family, her real blood family that was, even if it meant travelling half-way around the world. It was only right, wasn't it? Flora had been persistent with her questions for a while now and she, as her mother, had to face facts.

Perhaps her child's restless warring with those around her was part of her quest for knowing more of her roots.

Maybe I need to tell her more about her father, Delphi thought. But it has all been so delicate and painful. How do I tell her we were not married, that she is a bastard with all the shame that involves?

As she lay back in the deck lounger, Delphi stretched her arms high and took a deep intake of breath. Her home in Australia for the last ten years suddenly seemed remote. The die was cast when she had received that last letter from Papa saying how ill Rose had been. He had been very persuasive and had even sent her the money for the fare. She had supposed it was time to go and make her peace back there with her sister after all this time. She still had Flora, though, the evidence of the so-called sin she had performed. She hadn't regretted one moment of it despite the difficulties. Breathing out slowly she allowed the sun to seep into her soul. She closed her eyes. Yes this had to be the right thing to do, surely.

"May I sit here?" With the voice, Delphi became aware of a shadow across her face.

She opened her eyes and there was the lady who wore rather old-fashioned long flowered dresses she'd seen on boarding.

"Oh, I'm sorry my dear, I'm blocking out your sun. May I take this lounger?"

"Yes, by all means. Please do," Delphi answered.

"We met when we boarded although I don't expect you remember. You had your hands full with the little girl. Is it your young sister you're travelling with?" Without pausing for a response she continued. "We must have cabins close to each other. I mean, there're only fourteen of us in first, but I've not seen you during the last couple of days. I was laid low with sea sickness. Oh, I've never felt so ill. I do feel a bit better today though. I thought I'd make the effort. So . . . here I am"

Delphi was bewildered about which part of this diatribe to make comment.

"Listen to me rabbiting on and never a pause for breath. I'm not letting you get a word in edgeways."

There was much puffing and heaving as the lady sat down, arranged her flowing skirt and delved into a capacious tapestry bag for what emerged as some knitting.

"That's a pretty colour," Delphi said to be polite. After all they were going to be very close neighbours for some weeks and there was no-one else to whom she had spoken at any length. There was a middle-aged married couple who didn't seem too friendly, a few older men who looked as if they had formal business to attend to and then she and Flora had taken their first few meals in their cabin.

"It's for my granddaughter. I should have it finished by the time we dock back in the old country. Where's your little sister then?"

"She'll be lying on her bunk reading. She's always got her nose in a book. She's had to entertain herself all her life so she's very good at it. I think she'll run out of things to read long before we get to England." There was a pause. "I do have two sisters." Delphi frowned at the thought of that meeting to come, "but Flora's my daughter, not my sister," Delphi added.

"Oh sorry, I didn't mean to be . . . You don't look old enough. How old is she then? Nine? Ten? She's very pretty with her long dark hair. Takes after her mother, I can see."

"She's ten. Her name's Georgina but we call her Flora. It's a long story." She smiled. "My husband's name was George but he was killed on the Somme in 1916." The little lie tripped off her tongue as it had for the last nine years. In fact she had said it so often it seemed true and if George, her dear George, had lived . . .

Delphi wriggled in her chair and closed her eyes again. She could see jazzy swirls of colour through her lids and the warmth seeped in to relax her spirit at long last. The click-clack of knitting needles was a relentless but soothing metronome and she began to feel sleepy. The ship rode a gentle swell. She might have dozed off but then she felt a shadow pass between her and the sun again and she squinted up.

She couldn't quite see who it was standing there against the glare but his outline was blocking her sun and she wasn't pleased. Delphi became aware that she was frowning up at this stranger and brushing her hair away she tried to relax her forehead and put on a bit of a show just as she would have done in the old days. Some habits had never quite disappeared.

"Gooday, ladies," he said and touched his forelock. "It's a grand day for sitting out."

"Hello to you, young man," said Delphi's companion, saving her from speaking. "I don't believe we've been introduced. "I'm Mrs Shearer and this is . . . I'm sorry dear I don't even know your name."

"It's Delphi. Delphi Dight."

"And you're travelling with your little girl, Flora. Isn't that right?"

"Mmm"

"And I am Rainier, Rainier Harman. I don't believe I've had the pleasure yet. I didn't see you dining even. I would have remembered."

"I've not felt like eating anything these last couple of days. I've felt too ill," Mrs Shearer said.

"Poor you," The young man pulled a wry expression.

"Have you been ill too, Mrs Dight? We've not had the delight of your company either."

Delphi answered with coolness. He seems a bit smooth, she thought. "No, I've been fine. I chose to eat in my cabin with my daughter."

"Well, enjoy the sunshine, ladies. I hope we meet later."

By now Delphi's gaze had become more accustomed to the bright sun but she really only saw the man's broad shoulders and black hair curling on his collar as he retreated. He had a very strange accent she thought.

She huffed as she lay back again and tried to relax. Now though, she was feeling restless and pulling at the back of the lounger she sat more upright and looked out to sea. There were still a few birds following the ship but not many. She watched them idly as they tossed and swooped like pieces of white paper in their randomness. Otherwise the blue swell seemed vast and she with her worries and concerns suddenly felt small. Glancing across at her companion, she took in Mrs Shearer's substantial shape but also saw that as a result her skin was soft and downy. She had a mouth that was wide and generous and her bright blue eyes almost disappeared when she smiled but she was a comfortable companion. She must have become aware of the scrutiny and looked across at Delphi with a sparkle of wit.

"He's very attractive for a casual little fling." She gave a wicked grin. "Too young for me though. More your age I should say."

Delphi frowned at her. "I'm not in the running for any shipboard romance, that's for sure. There will only ever be one love for me and sadly he is no longer here," she added with an air of wistfulness. "I have Flora to consider too."

"Oh no, of course not, my dear. No harm in dreaming though." She winked across the narrow space between them.

Delphi shook her head and laughed. "I can see you are incorrigible and a force to be reckoned with, Mrs Shearer."

"You better call me Bea, if we are to be friends and neighbours. It's Beatrice of course but that sounds far too serious."

"Thank you, Bea."

Flora came scooting along the deck towards them, weaving a little with the movement of the ship. Her yellow dress swirled as she moved and reflected the butter colour onto her skin already burnished with fresh air and sun. Her hair shone and whisked around her elfin face as she brandished a book and grinned as she spied her mother. Introduction was made and she plonked herself down on the edge of Delphi's lounger.

"I've only got a few pages left. A very nice man just asked what I was reading," she said. "He said he has some books that I might borrow. He's going to France. That's where his folks are from, he said."

"We'll see what sort of books he's offering before we agree to that," Delphi said and Flora huffed at her.

I wonder if that was Rainier Harman. That must be why he speaks as he does, she thought. It's a weird mix of a French and Australian accent. She let out her breath. "Hmm." I don't know why I'm even bothering to think about it.

"I've read enough for the time being," Flora said. "What shall we do? They have deck games down there." She nodded towards the rear of the ship. Then putting her head on one side, her green eyes looked up at her mother through long lashes.

Delphi laughed at her. "You can stop looking at me like that my girl. I was the past master at wheedling things with a look like that so it won't work with me."

"Can you knit?" Bea Shearer held her work for Flora to see.

"No," she answered with a frown and peered at the cardigan that was emerging. "It looks very complicated."

"No it's really easy. Would you like me to show you how it's done? I've some spare needles in my bag."

So it was that Flora was occupied and Delphi was not when Rainier Harman came strolling by again.

Chapter 2

Delphi strolled along the deck, clasping her hands tightly in front of her.

"I was wondering, Mrs Dight, if you and your daughter would care to join my table at dinner tonight." Rainier said.

In order not to seem rude Delphi had agreed to walk with Mr Rainier Harman. Flora was fully engrossed in learning her new skill and Mrs Shearer was equally engaged. It had been difficult to invent a good excuse when he returned and asked if she would join him for a stroll around the deck. So here she was, desperately trying to think of a good reason not to agree to his invitation for this evening.

"Well, um. . ." She cast around her mind for an excuse. "Flora and I are happy to eat in our cabin," she said. "She's at an impressionable age and needs close supervision." Delphi could see further chasms of trouble between herself and Flora is the child started to form incorrect ideas about Delphi and her relationships. When Delphi had gone out to dinner with a local man back in Australia, there had been war to pay upon her return and for several days after. Delphi had not repeated the experiment.

"I'm sure but it's a long voyage and it was just a friendly suggestion."

Delphi felt mean and guilty for her response. He was trying to be gallant and affable. That was all. Bea Shearer's earlier flippant remarks had coloured her judgement. There was nothing flirtatious here, simply a good-natured gesture.

"Yes, of course. We should like to join you. Thank you and it's Delphi. Short for Delphinium but I hate that. My two sisters and I were all given flower names. The others are Rose and Iris but we call her Izzy."

They wandered on.

"Was it you who offered to lend Flora a book?"

"Yes. I have a few adventure stories that have travelled with me over the years. I have an ancient copy of Stevenson's '*The Black Arrow*'. I imagine she would devour it at her age. I had it as a boy and it's been with me ever since."

"It must have special meaning for you if you've had it that long," Delphi said.

"It's more the inscription in the front. My dad wrote it for me. It says 'Remember, my dear boy, that loyalty and duty are not always the same thing but honour remains constant.'
I know his words by heart I've read them so many times." He smiled to himself.

"That's very profound."

"It became significant along the Chemin des Dames in 1914 and especially in Ypres. My lungs are not quite the same since then. I like to think I did my duty and more. Loyalty was tested to the full." He looked away from her and out to sea.

Delphi looked at his profile for several seconds. "How old were you in 1914?"

"I was 17 and full of ideals about duty then. We learned," he finished and shrugged.

"Yes we all did. So you went to war before you were old enough, too." Delphi's thoughts strayed to her brother, Hector, before she continued. "She would love to read your book but only if you're sure. It sounds very precious."

"It has been but I'm going home now. Time to move on."

"Me too," she said. It slipped out and she could have slapped herself for allowing that. "Where is home?" She asked before he quizzed her about her own motives for returning to her family.

"My family home is a place in France. The nearest towns you might have heard of would be Amboise or Tours, of course, but my home is just south of there. We have vineyards and my father passed away recently. I've been studying wine production in Western Australia so it's time to return."

"I think you'll miss him. It sounds as if you were close."

"We were, in many ways, if not in miles."

"Why did you go so far away to study?" Delphi's curiosity was getting the better of her."

"I needed to get away; to have a change after the war; to travel and see life in a better way. Australia has some of the oldest grape varieties in the world. Many of Europe's established vineyards were destroyed by disease in 1800s, you know. So they had to import vines form Australia."

"That's ironic." Delphi laughed. "I've heard the French are zealous about their wine trade.

"Australia has some of the leading research centres in the world, too."

"I know, it's a major grower of vines, of course, but I lived on a ranch so that was very different." Here she was again, giving information about herself. She quickly moved on. "So you'll be disembarking at St Nazaire then?"

"That's right."

They stopped walking and Delphi rested her arms on the rails staring out to sea. The waves were a constant, rising and drawing away, scattering the light across their surface. Her mind drifted to the future and to seeing her sister Rose again after all these years. Would she have forgiven Delphi yet? Surely she would. Wouldn't she? It had all turned alright. She wondered how it would pan out now though. There so many unknowns. Her whole future was debatable but first she must see Rose and Michael too, of course. A shout from the group playing deck quoits brought her back.

"You were deep in thought there," Rainier said.

"Yes," Delphi answered. She did not elaborate but turned to retrace her steps.

***

He watched her slim retreating figure before stepping with long strides to catch her up.

"You're an enigma," he said.

She didn't respond.

"I've told you quite a bit about myself but you've managed to evade all my openings. What are you hiding or . . . of what are you afraid?" He asked with a sudden flash of insight.

"Me? I'm afraid of very little."

She flashed a brilliant smile in his direction and skipped a little turn in front of him, her dark auburn hair swinging out from her shoulders. Suddenly she was flirting, tilting her head and looking up at him with flashing green eyes. This was a completely different woman from the one at the railings. Now she was lively and sparkling. Her wide generous mouth laughed at him while she danced around. He wasn't fooled by this show of carelessness but he was enchanted and prepared to play along. This voyage could be fun with the little diversion of a beautiful woman along the way.

No ties, no seriousness. She seemed just the distraction to make time pass pleasantly and quickly. There was the slight complication of her daughter Flora but she was of an age to amuse herself and would be in bed early enough to make the evenings an entertaining game until the cat caught his little mouse. Not that this one was a mouse. Oh no, he could see that.

"You're a minx," he said and dimples appeared at the side of his wide mouth as he smiled, exposing strong, even teeth.

With that they returned to Bea Shearer and Flora who had mastered the basics of her knitting. She held up an uneven raggy looking strip with uncertain pride etched for all to see. Both Delphi and Rainier exclaimed their genuine pleasure at her achievement.

"That will make a fine scarf, or little skirt for one of your toys," he said and her frown dispersed.

"Thank you. I know mummy will say it's good whatever it looks like but if you think so too . . .," she said innocently.

"Oh I do indeed. By the way, your mother says you may borrow one of my books," Rainier added.

"Oh bees knees," Flora said in the slang of the day.

"Calm down," Delphi said and Flora shrugged her shoulders and tossed her head.

"Might she come and collect it now?" Rainier raised his eyebrows in a query at Delphi

"You leave that with me, Flora," said Bea, indicating the knitting. She winked at Delphi. "I'll just catch that dropped stitch. You all run along and I'll see you later."

"We'll walk that way together then," Delphi said as she picked up her own discarded book from the lounger.

As they arrived at the cabins Delphi and her daughter waited by their door while Rainier collected the book and gave it to Flora.

"What time would you like to go for dinner?"

They made arrangements.

"Are we eating in the restaurant tonight?" Flora asked. "Oh goody. I could wear my green dress at last, the one Gramps and Granny bought for me before we left." She turned to explain to Rainier. "We lived with them, didn't we Mummy."

"Come along now, that's enough chatter." Delphi took her arm gently and guided her towards their door.

"Mummy!" Flora shook her off.

Rainier stood watching as she opened the door of their cabin.

I bet she turns before going in, he thought.

Sure enough her eyes met his. He saw her breast heave with a sharp intake of breath as she surely realised he was still standing watching her with a smile twinkling across his face.

He imagined her thoughts as she disappeared, probably regretting giving him the satisfaction and being annoyed with herself.

He was looking forward to the evening.

Chapter 3

Delphi watched Flora prance and skip ahead of them as they lurched there way along the ship's passageway to the officer's mess where the first class cabin occupants ate. She could be so innocent and childlike one minute and tempestuous the next. It was the first time Delphi and Flora had been in here. The door was open but Rainier stood back to let them enter before him.

"All the tables are stuck to the floor," Flora said. "They've all got ledges around. Is that so things don't roll off?"

"Yes, that's right," Rainier answered. "You can imagine in rough weather things will slide around quite a bit."

"Including us." Flora laughed.

"Absolutely. We found it strange walking along to here just now and the sea's quite calm at the moment."

A member of the stewards came forward to show them to their seats, pulling one out for Delphi and spreading a crisp white napkin across her knees before helping her to tuck under the table. Rainier did the same for Flora.

"There you are ma'am," he said looking down at her and smiling.

She wriggled and preened. Delphi smiled across the table at him appreciating he was making this first dinner in the mess special for her daughter.

"You're looking particularly lovely tonight," he said to the child. "That shade of green suits you and you're tall so the fashion is very becoming. You, Delphi, look stunning."

She felt warmth rise up her neck and was annoyed with herself but it was a long time since she had been out with a man, if this could be called 'out' and she was relieved that Flora was enjoying his company too.

As she had on the deck earlier, she recognised recklessness bubbling up. This feeling she had in adolescence which had ultimately been her undoing she squashed down. He better not try coming on to her, though. Eating in the mess would be more interesting since they were on board for several weeks but that's all. She had Flora of whom to be aware and the child was demanding beyond most of her age. Glancing at her daughter now, a rush of love burst through from her stomach to the tip of her toes and out through her lovely face in a dazzling smile. Flora, unaware of her mother's gaze, broke her bread roll trying to look grown-up and worldly.

When Delphi dragged her eyes away and looked across the table, Rainier was staring at her intently. She turned her head quickly to look out of the porthole next to her. When she returned her face to look again which she could not resist, he was still looking at her.

To hide her confusion, putting her head coquettishly on one side, she said "So Rainier, tell me. . ." she thought with agitation, "Tell me of the life you will lead when you return home."

Phew, she relaxed, now on safer territory again.

"The house is old, very old. It's been in my family for a couple of hundred years. There's only about ten hectares of vines but we produce mainly white wine from the chenin grape although we call it pineau blanc and, sauvignon blanc too. It's thriving."

"We better drink white tonight then," Delphi said.

The first course, little pieces of fish in a delicious sauce with small toasts and garnish on the side, came and went and conversation was light like the wine. The main course was goujons of chicken and so the alcohol was a perfect match even though the choice was limited aboard ship and not French, of course.

Delphi began to relax.

While they ate Rainier was the perfect host and asked Flora what hobbies she enjoyed and what her favourite subjects at school were. He studiously avoided questions about why they had lived in Australia or where they were heading and for what reason. Delphi was relieved and grateful.

"Good evening, dears," said Bea Shearer as she swayed into the mess. "I thought I'd give in here a try since I feel so much better. I think I've found my sea legs at last."

Rainier stood.

"Will you join us?" he asked gallantly.

"Oh no but that's very kind. You're well along the way and I shall hold you up. I'll sit over there." She tottered across the room holding a table edge here and a chair back there to steady herself. Her copious bosom heaved as she took a deep breath and collapsed into the seat held out for her by the steward. She waved across at them and smiled.

Having finished their dessert and while sitting quietly for a while with coffee, Bea came across to their table.

"I'm not having dessert or coffee. Why don't I take Flora to her bed? I could read to her and you folks can have a gentle stroll on deck before saying goodnight." She winked at Delphi.

"Oh you don't need to do that," Delphi said, suddenly feeling trapped.

"That would be grand." Flora looked up at the older lady. "I've started the book Mr Harman gave me, '*The Black Arrow.*' Do you know it?"

"Oh my goodness me, yes. It's really good and quite exciting."

Flora pushed her chair back.

"That's alright isn't it, Mummy?" Delphi couldn't believe that Flora was being so flexible but despite her pleasure in this she gave a tight smile. She didn't need to be left in this position with Rainier Harman.

"Go on then, Sweetie. Teeth and bed in good order. Love you," she added when she saw a look flit across Flora's face when she realised her mother was not totally in agreement.

She watched her child and the older lady, who clutched her young one's arm, as they lurched across the floor.

"It's a very long time since I was on board a ship," Delphi said. "I hope we don't have too much rough weather this voyage."

But the wind had died as it often does in early evening, and all was calm, including Delphi's raging thoughts for once. Perhaps it was the wine.

***

Rainier left the table and helped her stand. She preceded him from the mess but staggered herself as the ship rode a particularly big wave. He caught her before she hit the bulkhead too hard and kept his arm under hers as they headed for the outside. She felt his warmth seeping through her.

Whilst there were only a small number of first class passengers there were more than seven hundred third class people so the deck was busy since it was a fine night. Gone were the days of segregation to the extent of the famous and infamous ships of the White Star line of the first decades of the century.

"It's busy here. Let's go up one."

"We'd have been third class if Papa had not sent me the money for the ticket. I wouldn't have minded sharing a cabin with someone like Bea."

Rainier guided Delphi to the quieter area and they leaned on the railing. Despite the fading light the sun cast hues of pink and palest orange and pearl across the horizon. The sea rose and fell and the ship rolled with it.

"So, will you tell me?"

"Tell you what?"

She's pretending again, he thought. Pretending not to know to what I refer.

"Where you're going and why. Where you are running from."

"I'm not running away, definitely not that," she said.

He stood leaning on the railing next to her and said nothing.

"Please smoke if you wish," Delphi said.

"I don't smoke," he answered, "Not since the war. I had a brush with some gas but fortunately it wasn't bad. It's just left me with a patch on my lung so I have to be a bit careful." He chuckled. "Hey, you've got me talking about myself again. Tell me something about you. Anything. A scrap of information which helps me to know you better."

She sighed.

"Very well. I was happy in Australia. I lived with my husband's parents and had Flora there with them."

The little lie tripped from her mouth again but it was only a small one.

"I'm going home to see my family again. My sister, Rose, has been very ill with TB."

"I see. Australia was a long way for you to go to have a child. Tell me, please, what happened to your husband?" He spoke so that Delphi hardly heard him.

She said nothing for a long while and Rainier stood beside her patiently until he wondered whether she had heard his question.

"George was killed. On the Somme. My brother-in-law was his best friend and they were together except Michael survived."

"You must have been very young."

"Yes well, it was war wasn't it. Things happen."

He looked at her quizzically but she said no more.

"Have you not been home in all this time?"

"No. My sister and I had a major falling out. Still, she's been so ill and Papa was very persuasive. Flora needs to meet her family too. She's been asking. Things have not been easy for her and she rebels quite often. I think she must be in a muddle about whom she is and where she belongs."

"Your in-laws will miss you back in Oz."

"My father-in-law died last year and my mother-in-law will go and live with her daughter so she'll be fine. I think she'll sell up the ranch. It's too much now anyway; managing all the hands and the finances. She'll miss Flora in some ways but probably not in others."

"Anyone would miss Flora. She's a credit to you."

Delphi looked up into his eyes and allowed herself to smile. "She's been particularly amenable to you. She can be a little demon if she doesn't like someone."

She saw him regarding her and by the deck lights she noticed the crinkles at the corners of his warm brown eyes and his white teeth as he smiled back. A tremble somewhere deep inside surprised her and she felt wobbly. His shoulders were broad and he was tall. His hair curling onto his collar was unfashionably long, but it suited him well. She caught a whiff of lemon and something else cleanly honest and earthy from his clothing. She recognised her feelings but resolutely quashed them. Flora needed consideration. He would disappear from her life in three or four weeks. She was independent and had been for nine years. What she didn't need was a romance, never mind a short term affair. She knew where that could lead. Although George had been the one love of her life, it caused her major upheaval and problems and yes, she did still miss him desperately. She did *not* need a man.

"So, Delphi Dight, exciting times ahead for both of us," Rainier said, lightening the mood.

"Would you like a night-cap before we part? I have a bottle of exceptionally good whisky in my room. Don't panic. I saw the look in your eyes just then. I shall it fetch here. I have no wish to compromise you. I think you may be a girl who would appreciate a man's drink, though." He winked at her and laughed.

She relaxed again. "Thank you. That would be lovely."

Returning with the bottle and two glasses Rainier stood in the shadows for a moment and watched her. She was certainly a complex baggage but her lithe figure sheathed in the silk of her evening dress was very alluring. She had an exotic look with her high cheek bones and slanting eyes and her long dark hair was different to the bobbed hair-cut of so many women of the day.

She threw back her head, as he watched, the better to take the evening breeze, he supposed, and her long neck with the contour of her small Adam's apple was pale and inviting. He said he had no wish to compromise her but he did. God how he did. He felt himself grow stiff so waited a moment longer. Apart from anything else, she was a challenge and that he admired. She had a past, the detail of which he could only guess but it certainly did not deter him.

He cleared his throat which had become tight with his erection and moved towards her, thankful for the dark that had descended.

"Shall we find a seat?" he asked.

They moved together and he poured for her as she sat sideways on a lounger in the shadow of the bulkhead and out of the stiffening breeze.

"Here's to our future lives." He raised his glass and she held hers until his met and they clinked together like a gentle seduction.

Chapter 4

Delphi and Rainier shared many such evenings while Bea often kept an eye on Flora, either reading to her or helping with the ever-growing knitting. Delphi became more confident in her friendship with him and felt less need to be false and flirtatious. She learned of his home life in France and in turn she told him of her adolescence in England and a little about each of her sisters and their parents. She didn't tell him about George and her relationship with Flora's father. As far as he and the rest of the world were concerned they had been married, albeit for a short time and he had been killed just after when she was already expecting his child. Australia was far enough away from all she knew for that to work.

This particular afternoon they stood on the games deck. They had laughed such a lot. Rainier played the fool for Flora's benefit, running around balancing the quoit on his head and pretending he couldn't find it; using the shuffle stick as a wooden leg and acting like a pirate. Delphi had watched and wondered at a man who was so unafraid of making himself absurd for a nine-year old and appreciating the fact. In front of her too, whom she knew he was trying hard to impress.

"I think the weather's on the turn," Delphi said looking out at the ridge of cloud approaching and feeling the wind across her face.

"One more game of shuffleboard?" Flora had the pleading look that Delphi knew so well.

"Just one then. It'll be time to get ready for dinner soon."

Delphi looked forward to dinners in the mess. The habit of sitting with Rainier and seeing the appreciative look in his eyes was appealing after so many years living miles from civilisation like a nun. She felt powerful and confident. His eyes watched her. She knew she was good-looking. It had been a curse in her adolescence. But now she liked his eyes, following her. She liked his eyes; dark brown and soulful one moment and sparkling with vitality the next. She appreciated his physique too. His shoulders were broad and his hips were narrow. Often his shirt came untucked from the back of his trousers but still he managed to look suave and handsome. Well, she thought so anyway.

Having finished their game they collected the pucks and moved to stow their sticks in the box. The sea became more choppy by the minute and the cloud cover was flat and grey. Wind blew Delphi's hair around her face and she pushed it back from her eyes. She shivered in the stiff breeze. Gazing across from port side she saw white tops to the waves and an uneven heaviness about it all.

They needed to balance carefully as they went back to their cabin. Rainier's arm came around Delphi on more than one occasion to steady her.

"You come between us, Flora and we can steady you." Delphi manoeuvred across.

"I'm fine. This is fun. It's a bit like being at that funfair we went to on holiday. Do you remember?" She skipped ahead.

That night Delphi was awoken by Flora.

"Mummy I feel sick."

Delphi leaped up to find a towel, pushing her hair from her bleary face and to guide Flora into the bathroom where the child made it just in time to lean over the wash-hand basin before she heaved up her dinner.

The ship pitched up and down and rolled from side to side. Delphi hung onto the handle beside the basin and steadied Flora at the same time as trying to maintain her balance.

"I don't like it, I'm scared," said Flora between being ill. Her face was pasty and pale and her neck was damp with wisps of hair clinging to that and her cheeks.

"Nothing to be scared about," Delphi said grabbing the tin waste paper basket on her way back to the bunk to which she guided Flora. Her own stomach was rising and falling with the motion but she didn't feel sick. She never had. For that she was very grateful right now.

The noise was phenomenal. Each time the ship pitched forwards there was a loud thumping bang. The waved lashed the portholes and the wind whined through wires outside and sounded eerie.

There was a crashing sound from nearby.

"That sounded like it came from Bea's cabin," she said to Flora. I hope she's alright."

"Mummy, don't leave me," came a pitiful cry from the bunk.

"I'm not going anywhere, sweetie. Hush now. Don't cry." She stroked her daughter's sweaty hair-line. "I'm going to get a damp flannel, that's all."

Delphi hurried to the bathroom, reeling across the floor from one side to the other and managed to avoid all manner of things that had fallen off the side and were rolling about. A dribble of salt water ran from the porthole-casing as a wave crashed against it and the ship shuddered. The vessel, sliding bow down, and the immense banging and juddering that was indeed very frightening, continued.

"Mummy," Flora called and Delphi made her weaving way back.

The night wore on in repetitive noise and shaking with an exhausted child in turn retching and moaning. Delphi's heart was thumping and her stomach was tense with upset for her child but not with sea sickness.

Slowly the porthole took on a lighter shade as the day dawned grim and grey but still the wild sea crashed and smashed against it. Flora dozed at last but Delphi could not.

There was a tentative knock at her door.

She staggered across to open it and peer through the crack, clutching her dressing gown across her rumpled nightclothes.

***

Delphi stood before Rainier. Her face was pale and her lovely green eyes were huge with grey beneath them. His heart went out to her for the worry and discomfort engraved there. As he stood, the ship was flung down again and he put his hand out to steady himself.

"You look done in," he said. "Are you ill?"

"No but Flora is. I've been up all night so I'm a bit raggy round the edges."

"Is there anything I can do? You look so weary."

"Is Bea alright? Do you know? I heard such a crash earlier but I couldn't leave Flora."

"I went in and helped her up. She fell against the desk on her way to the bathroom. She'll have a huge bruise, I think, but I believe nothing's broken. I sat with her for a while. She's been very ill too but she's quieter now so I said I'd check on you. All's fine, so if there's. . ."

As the ship lurched again in a different direction, Delphi clung to the door and it shot open as she was flung back. She dropped the front of her dressing gown as she struggled to remain upright, grabbing at the door with her other hand.

Rainier stepped forward. He placed strong arms around her for support and at the same time pulled her clothing across to protect her. Although his eyes strayed and he gasped, he managed not to betray his interest more than that. He had seen enough to know that, although she was lithe, she was full-breasted and he imagined large, dark nipples and skin unmarked by any blemishes. She was very desirable.

This would be so easy to take advantage, he thought, but strangely all he wanted was for her to be safe and content again.

He guided her to a chair and sat her down. She was soft and compliant. Brushing her hair from her face he turned to the bunk where Flora was stirring again.

"Mummy," she murmured.

"Ssh, she's here but she's really tired. I think you better have some water but not a great gulp."

He put his arm behind her hot little body and raised her head. Holding the cup he let her take a sip but wouldn't allow her much.

"I'm thirsty," she whispered.

"I know but take several small mouthfuls rather than a lot at once. You're tummy will be tender."

He turned to look at Delphi for confirmation of what he was doing but she lay in the chair with her eyes closed. He didn't know if she slept but he took the flannel and indicated to Flora that he was going into the bathroom to refresh it.

On returning, Flora started heaving again but nothing much came up. He wiped her face and lay her down again.

"Thank you," she murmured.

He pulled the other chair to the bedside and sat, happy to be of practical assistance. Looking across at Delphi again he wondered what her life had been like. He had learned that she had lived with her in-laws and it appeared there had been no other man on the scene. She was capable yet vulnerable; independent yet frightened of any advancement he might have tried in those early days.

He was aware that he must be falling in love. He had not felt this way before. Women were for enjoyment and fun, nothing too serious or anchoring. As he watched her, he felt tenderness and desire. He wanted her body but he yearned for her soul. As he had these thoughts he was startled by them.

He put his head in his hands. Why this? Why now? He had to disembark at St Nazaire. His family loyalty and duty awaited and could not be postponed.

He had put duty above loyalty in 1914. There had been a heavy price to pay then although not as great as some of his friends. Had he to do the same again now?

But he knew the answer.

Chapter 5

The night of the balloon dance was imminent.

"It's going to be so exciting," Flora could hardly sit still while thinking about it. "Are you looking forward to it too?"

"I certainly am," Delphi said.

"I'm so glad I can go, even if it's only for a short while. Tell me again about the balloons."

"It's only what I've heard but I believe there will be hundreds all over the floor and decorating the walls tied to the lamp brackets."

"Will there be all colours?"

"I told you before." She laughed. "As far as I know"

In reality Delphi had very mixed feelings. It would be a great diversion. The voyage had become tedious in many ways with lazy days, stormy interludes, deck games. But the evenings were charged with sexual tension from which Delphi had tried to distance herself yet found that hard too.

"We've been at sea for so long, now, the dance'll be fun," she said.

"The only thing is . . ." Flora hesitated before she continued." It means Rainier will be leaving the ship in a couple of days. I'll miss him. Will you miss him Mummy?"

Delphi became breezy and brittle in her response. "Of course but he has a big experience to go to so we must be pleased for him. It won't be long after that until we dock too and we'll be ready for our next adventure. Now let's plan what we shall wear."

When they entered the grand salon the next night the lights were settling a soft lambent hue on everything else. It transformed the room from the common place to the land of magic. Glasses caught the sparkle, the furniture was burnished to a rich deep shine and the floor was covered in a thousand balloons singing of every tone and shade imaginable.

Flora stood in the doorway and clasped her hands together.

***

Rainier spotted Delphi and her daughter as soon as they stood framed in the doorway. The magical radiance reflected on them both.

They are captivating, magnificent, he thought. Flora looked like a smaller version of her mother but wearing green and with much innocence in her smiling face as she clasped her hands together.

The aura of Delphi in her peacock blue gown seemed to whisper across the room to him. He was overwhelmed and could do nothing but stand and gape. She had her hair piled up emphasising her long neck. That white skin that had affected him so. Her figure, silhouetted, aroused him afresh. Her spirit seeped across the space between them and all else faded to silence until there was only the two of them facing each other.

Then Flora left her mother and came floating towards him through the balloons. He put his arms out to give her a hug and she snuggled into him with confidence. Lifting her head she looked at him and said, "This is the best night ever, in the whole world."

"Yes, it is," he said smiling down at her.

Taking her hand, Rainier moved towards Delphi and reached out for her. She placed her hand in his and together the three of them crossed the room to take a seat.

"I've never danced among so many balloons before," Delphi said as Rainier held her for a quickstep and they did a spin turn in the corner. It wasn't the easiest thing to do in such a confined space and there was the occasional bang as a balloon was trodden by an eager dancer. There were far more men than women among the first class passengers and senior crew so not many dancing. There were several uniformed men standing around the edges, holding glasses of drink. Delphi was aware of eyes following her even though they were nodding with each other in conversation. She was used to it.

"They're all the rage apparently. The first officer told me," Rainier shouted in her ear.

"Sorry?" she shouted back.

"The balloons. They're very popular at such events as this."

What with the noise of chatter and the loud music it was difficult to converse.

He shuffled around the room with Flora and once or twice with Bea. The older lady and the child sat together now and watched Rainier and Delphi who made a striking couple, both being tall and handsome.

"It's like dancing in a dry mist of colour." Delphi lifted her right hand from his shoulder and held her skirt as they spun again.

"It's soft globes of enchantment." He looked down at her and smiled.

"You're quite the poet."

"When I'm inspired." He smiled.

The next dance was a waltz and without asking if she'd had enough he glided her back and forth and around and around. He pressed his hand on the small of her back and as she turned her head to the left he felt the whole length of her body close to his. If she stood any closer she would feel his hardness.

"Oh, Delphi," he murmured into her hair but he didn't know if she'd heard him.

The music ended and they pulled apart. Rainier took her hand to guide her back to Bea and Flora who sat around the low table they had commandeered at the beginning of the evening.

"What a handsome couple you make," Bea said.

"You do look lovely when you dance, Mummy."

"Thank you," Delphi said.

She was distracted by the First Officer who asked for the next dance and then another gentleman claimed her. She had to refuse the third because she was gasping for a drink.

Rainier watched as others spun her round or tried to hold her close. He was troubled and he knew exactly why.

***

Two days later Delphi and Flora shared the air of expectancy among the crew and the passengers. France had been in sight for quite some time and now they were heading up the mighty River Loire into the busy port of St Nazaire.

The passengers who were not disembarking leaned on the railings to watch the activities of the bank slide by.

"What's that?" Flora pointed her finger at a skeleton hull away to the side.

"Apparently it's a new ship being built. That's the SS Ile de France, Miss," said a passing sailor.

"Where's Rainier, Mummy? He's missing all this."

"He'll be packing the last of his things, darling." Delphi put her arm around her child. She felt in need of comfort.

They were travelling really slowly now. They passed a large building with a tall chimney belching smoke. Delphi could easily see the time on the clock telling her that sadness was imminent.

As they manoeuvred and turned someone said "There's *le Pont Tournant*. It's not old but opens to let water traffic through."

"Will be going through there?" Flora turned her face up to Delphi.

"No we shan't be going that way."

Rainier arrived by her side. He had some hand luggage with him reminding her of his departure. This must be born with fortitude. She had suffered worse in the past but at this moment she was close to weeping. She hadn't felt like this for nearly ten years and hadn't believed she would ever again until recently.

The business of tying up alongside the quay seemed to take forever. There was clanking and shouting of orders. Bumping and shuddering sent waves of nausea through Delphi and she became light-headed.

I want to tell him things. I want to share my feelings but it's no good now. I can't share the circumstances of Flora's birth. He'll know what I was, what I am, what Rose said I was. Society doesn't forgive that and neither will he. It's better this way. . . But oh, how it hurts.

Tears were very close to brimming and rolling down her lovely face.

She'd come so close to committing the same sin after the dance the other night but had managed somehow to withhold her true feelings.

Now, very aware of his every breath, his every movement by her side, she gritted her teeth.

She felt his arm steal around her waist.

"Oh Delphi, this is awful. You know how I feel," he said at last.

"I do know."

"I have my duty to perform and you have something you need to complete too, I think."

"Yes."

"And still you have not confided everything," he said giving a small bitter laugh.

"Rainier, I can't. Not here, probably not ever."

"This is goodbye then, my dearest. Will you walk with me to the top of the gangplank?"

"Bea will you watch Flora for me one more time?" There was a pleading in her eyes.

"Of course. You go along. We'll watch from here."

"Thank you so much. I shan't be long and then, Flora, we can wave bye-bye from up here together."

Rainier gave Flora a quick hug and shook Bea's hand warmly before kissing her soft plump cheek. She had tears in her eyes.

"I hate goodbyes. Go on with you and God speed, my dear boy."

Together Rainier and Delphi shuffled and pushed through the crowds amassed between the railings and the bulkhead towards the gangplank which was now firmly in place. It was awkward as he carried his bag and there was such a press of people.

The last moment arrived for him to go; the dreaded time. He dropped his bag and enfolded her whether she wanted him to or not. He kissed her full on the lips with passion and longing. Then he turned. Before she realised and appreciated the full impact, he grabbed his hold-all and left.

Delphi watched his tall retreating frame. She took a step forward and put out her arm.

Just once he turned and then he was gone from her life, she thought.

Chapter 6

Plymouth, their disembarkation port, was a still a very long way from Papa's house and they must catch a train to Manchester where he would meet them with the motor car.

The porter and the taxi driver were very helpful and soon they were installed in a carriage. Luggage would follow.

Delphi's mind was bubbling and her heart was pounding as the train pulled away. Very soon her view of countryside was excluded by steep tree-clad banks which trapped the steam from the engine and blew it past the carriage windows. The pungent odour of it crept into their nostrils. Even this brought nostalgic memories flooding. It wasn't long before a wide sky and rolling hills drew their sight. She had been so looking forward to the fresh smells of the English countryside and to seeing the rolling hills of her youth. Now, she was confused and uncertain.

"Mummy look," Flora said. "There're sheep but so few of them. And look at those houses. Aren't they funny? But they have an upstairs and no veranda. It's all so different."

Delphi regarded the scenery, so alien after her years away, and yet so comforting too. She longed to be out in the northern hills, striding along and breathing the cool clean air without the dust and dryness to which she had become accustomed. She doubted she would ride a horse again in a long while but then she wouldn't need to. Not that she had ridden much. That was men's occupation. Hers had been in the homestead helping her mother-in-law.

What would life hold for her now? It would be so different and strange. Never normally fearful, she suddenly was breathless and uncomfortable.

She sat back and closed her eyes, willing the motion of the carriage lull her back to calmness and expectancy rather than alarm and apprehension.

"I wonder what Rainier's doing." Flora's voice interrupted her thoughts.

"I'm sure he's excited as we are to be back with his family," Delphi answered, trying to sound positive and avoiding her daughter's eyes as she gazed across the hills.

I wonder, indeed, she thought.

"Tell me again about when you were a girl."

Delphi smiled at Flora. "How many times have you heard this?"

"I want to picture what it'll be like when we live with Grandpapa," the child said.

"As you know Rose, me and Izzy . . ."

Delphi launched into the descriptions of herself and her two sisters growing up, yet again.

***

After Flora, Delphi climbed into her father's car outside the train station with trepidation. In a short time she would be going to meet her sister Rose. The first time in nearly ten years was on her mind more than seeing everyone else and it was unsettling to say the least. Izzy had been too young to really know what had gone on and it had not had any effect on her anyway. Some others in the household knew of her disgrace, of course, but not of the row between her older sister and herself or the reason for it. That had stayed between them. The bitter words Rose had used which were so uncharacteristic of her had stayed branded in Delphi's mind with all their searing red-hot rage.

"We'll go home," her father said. "Get you settled in. Izzy is dying to see you again."

I wonder how much that is true, Delphi thought. Still she's older now. Perhaps she's forgotten how horrid I could be to her when we were young. As she sat there next to Flora she was transported back. The smell of pipe tobacco and Papa's toilet water had not changed. She suddenly felt all her childhood insecurities again.

"As for Dora," her father continued, seemingly unaware of the turmoil she felt. "She has hardly been able to contain her impatience. She stays in her room for most of the time and copes with the mending and such-like. I think she enjoys the peace but if she ventures down to the kitchen she tends to interfere with things and the new maid, Betty, gets quite short with her. Izzy's had to sort out more than one row."

So many memories and too many changes since she last stepped over the threshold had robbed Delphi of composure.

She forced down her feelings. "How is Izzy?"

"She's well. Since returning from her spell in Germany she has her charity work and her little groups."

Poor Izzy, Delphi thought. That all sounds very dull. The fate of the youngest sister, left at home to tend her widower father.

"She hasn't been back long though has she? I thought from your last letter she was enjoying her stay there."

"She was but she was happy to come home to see you when I told her you were coming. After all, she has been there some time. I'm sure her wider education was more or less complete."

Flora had sat silently until now. Delphi knew she was shy of this other grandpa that she had never met and did not know.

"And Aunt Rose? How is Aunt Rose doing and how is Uncle Michael managing the school without her?" Flora plucked up her courage to ask the question that Delphi had put off asking but was desperate to know. Delphi smiled at her daughter who was so unaware of all the complex relationships of the past.

"Rose has been very poorly, as you know but I do believe she's on the mend. She looks like a shadow, though. I think you'll see quite a difference in her, Delphi." Papa was concentrating on the road ahead but he glanced over his shoulder at his daughter. "You must be brave and school your face not to let your shock or surprise show, my dear. Flora, you won't mind staying with Izzy when we go to visit, will you? They won't allow children into the sanatorium." He drove on in silence and did not address the second part of Flora's question.

Delphi patted Flora's hands which were held together tightly in her lap.

Eventually Delphi could wait no longer. "And the school?"

"Oh, Michael's employed a senior mistress while Rose is away. That great mausoleum of a place is very draining both financially and in every other way, I believe. He doesn't say a lot, not to me anyway. I have a feeling his father has been helping out a bit. The bills must be extraordinary just for heating the place. Since the Duke of Norfolk entrusted the building I think there's an agreement that he'll continue with maintenance for the time being. The roof alone must cost a fortune to keep watertight."

"Why on earth did they take such a place?"

"Well, Delphi, you'll see eventually. It is beautiful and has all the facilities they need to develop the school into the sort of place that will command high fees. It's been improving very nicely but then this blow of Rose's illness and all that worry has had an effect on everything. Still, parents of pupils seem very loyal so I suppose that's some sort of testament to how they feel about the whole setup."

Delphi said no more. She wanted to confide her nervousness of seeing Rose again but not in front of her daughter.

"So what about you, young lady?" Flora's grandpa stretched his neck to see her in his driving mirror. "Big changes, eh? How was that long voyage?"

"It was fine, thank you. Rainier lent me some books and we played deck games. I didn't like the storms though."

"She was very seasick I'm afraid, weren't you?" Delphi turned to her daughter.

"And who is Rainier?"

"He was a very nice friend on the ship," Flora answered.

"Was he your age?" Grandpa Strong asked.

Flora giggled. "Oh no. He was Mummy's friend.

Her Papa looked back at Delphi again. "Oh I see," he said.

Delphi could not hold his gaze.

***

This visit with Rose felt such a contrast with meeting the rest of the people back at the house the day before.

Izzy had come running down the stairs as soon as the front door opened. Delphi would not have known her. She had changed so, grown into a woman, and at twenty years of age was quite a beauty. She had Rose's fine hair but her colouring was that of Delphi. Whilst she did not have the high cheek bones and slanting eyes that were Delphi's alone she had the same heart-shaped face and she was elfin and very pretty.

"Delphi!" She swooped upon her elder sister and hugged her with enthusiasm, dismissing Delphi's own anxiety that Izzy might resent her return after so long. She always did have a sweet nature.

"It's good to be back."

"Listen to you. You have a definite twang to your accent now. And you must be Flora." She turned and put her hand on Flora's arm. It's so good to meet you."

Dora enveloped Delphi. "My darling child. It's very good to see you."

Then the elderly retainer had enfolded Flora and the child had all but disappeared into the ample bosom. "Little Flora, you are most welcome. I've been so looking forward to meeting you." She turned to Delphi. "A child in the house again. What could be better?"

"Welcome, Mrs Dight. Pleased to meet you and you Miss Dight," said Betty. Let me get you some lemonade. You must be tired and thirsty."

Dora 'harrumphed' at that but Izzy asked her to join them all in the salon so she was mollified.

Now Delphi climbed out of the car in front of the sanatorium and her Papa held her arm while he closed the door after her. Together they climbed steps up to a large and heavy-looking door with a bell mechanism to one side which Papa pulled twice. Somewhere deep inside she could just here the results. The door opened and a nurse in a white uniform with an old fashioned white headdress smiled at them. She looked more like a nun from the last century than a modern nurse, Delphi thought.

"Mr Strong, Ma'am." She nodded her head at them and stood back to let them in. "Mrs Rose is sitting in the conservatory today. She had a good night. Would you like me to accompany you?"

"Thank you. This is Rose's sister, Mrs Dight. She's come all the way from Australia."

"My goodness, Mrs Dight that is a long way. Your sister will be ever so pleased to see you, I'm sure."

We'll see, thought Delphi but simply smiled and nodded.

The corridors were long and painted like any other hospital; duck egg blue below the dark green dado and cream above. The walls were blank and uninteresting.

The odd picture here and there might help, Delphi thought.

In one corner there was a plant on a table that someone a long time ago had placed, presumably trying to make the place seem more homely but it looked tired. Delphi knew some patients were here for months while doctors sought to cure damaged lungs.

Doors with glass panes led off on one side but every so often there were small sitting rooms with high backed chairs and occasional tables. One or two patients appeared to be ensconced. Some were dozing and some reading.

"May we speak to a doctor before we go to see my daughter?" Mr Strong glanced at Delphi. "Mrs Dight here would really like to know first-hand how she is progressing and what treatment is being administered."

"Of course, Mr Strong. Perhaps you would like to sit in here. It's specifically for visitors rather than patients. They use the corridor on the other side," she said by way of explanation to Delphi. The nurse opened a door and ushered them into a small room, sparsely but comfortably furnished.

"The condition is very contagious, Delphi. There is a strict protocol here about visitors and patients being kept separate."

"I know so little. I feel a bit helpless," Delphi said.

"It was a long time before Rose was permitted any visitors," said her father. "Michael was beside himself with worry but fortunately, by some miracle, he hasn't caught it. The school was quarantined for quite a while though. Things have been very, very difficult."

Delphi sat and fidgeted. Then she stood and paced before sitting again. The door opened and a man in a white coat entered. Delphi thought his smile aimed at being encouraging but it didn't dispel her anxiety about the forth-coming meeting with Rose.

"Mr Strong and . . . Mrs Dight?" His voice held a questioning inflection.

"Yes, I'm Rose's sister." Delphi held out her hand. The doctor's was warm and his smile lit his face.

"It's good to meet you. Your sister is making steady progress."

"I know it's a killer, this disease. Will she survive?" We have unfinished issues to resolve, Delphi thought to herself. Please, God, let's be able to do that. Then she felt selfish. Rose's health and her future should be far more important than Delphi's petty needs.

"I am confident now that your sister will live. It was not like that at first though and she will always have a weakness of the lungs. She must be careful not to get over-tired in the future and any colds and coughs will have to be monitored carefully."

"What treatment does she have?"

Plenty of fresh air now. We had to collapse her lung to rest it, at first. There is little else we can do. She's very lucky indeed."

"I thought there was some sort of injection."

"No. In France experiments continue and there seems to have been some success with a vaccination to prevent catching the disease but I'm afraid we are nowhere near a medical cure yet," the doctor said.

"I see," Delphi said, feeling helpless again.

"Take heart, Mrs Dight. Your sister is getting better. It's been a long process but she is one of the lucky ones." The doctor sounded confident. "Would you like to come now? I know Rose is looking forward to seeing you. She has spoken of you a lot and I can see why now," he added quietly. He seemed to be speaking to her alone and her Papa excluded. Then she was used to this attention from men. Hadn't it got her into trouble with Rose all those years ago?

Chapter 7

Papa preceded Delphi into the conservatory, holding the door for her as she passed him. It was hot and felt steamy and smelled not unpleasantly of damp moss but as she moved forwards she felt a breeze and realised that huge vents above were open as were the double doors at one end.

And there she was. Rose. Sitting on her own with a slant of sun striking the floor beside her as she read a book.

She always was studious and so clever, thought Delphi. That was a problem too. I was jealous and envious of the opportunities she had. But then that was my fault. I know that now. I could have gone to college too if I'd wanted but I was childish, resentful and flighty. I should have stuck to my studies as Rose did. I didn't appreciate how forward thinking Papa was in letting us learn as we did.

Delphi stood for a moment partly shielded by a large fern. She watched and took a moment to process what she saw. Rose, always small, looked shrunken in the capacious wicker seat. Her fly-away hair was neat, of course, but her glasses kept slipping down and she pushed them up again as she read.

Then Delphi felt the doctor's hand on her arm and she turned her face to him. He smiled and nodded his encouragement.

He knows my feelings, she thought. He seems to understand my turmoil.

She looked again into his dark eyes and thought of Rainier. If only he was here with her now. He would know how she felt too. She should have told him everything when she had the opportunity. He may have understood even her most heinous sin. He had been to war. He knew what it was like and how rich emotions were back then. And now it was too late. He was gone from her life. He had responsibilities and so did she. She closed her eyes momentarily and took a deep breath.

"Rose my dear," she said as she stepped forward from the shelter of the greenery.

Rose looked up and smiled and there was her sister, the Rose she knew, though tired and frail. There were dark circles beneath her eyes but a light from within shone out. She closed her book and placing it on the table she struggled out of her chair.

"Doctor Brown, Benjamin, says I am no longer contagious." She opened her arms. "Oh Delphi, my dear sister. How we have missed you," she said.

Delphi went forwards and received the benediction of Rose's kiss on her cheek.

"We have much to talk about," Rose said, "But suffice for now that you're here and I'm getting better. We have lots of time to get to know each other all over again."

"There's so much I need to say to you, Rose."

"I know and I too but as I say we have plenty of time."

She was always seeing the good in people, always looking for the reasons for my bad behaviour, Delphi thought. She always tried to forgive but it didn't serve her well to be self-effacing all the time.

"Let's just enjoy being together and I do want to know all about Flora. I'm so looking forward to meeting her. Papa thank you for coming to see me again." Rose accepted his kiss on her forehead. "Delphi come and sit here next to me and we'll ask a special favour and see if we can have tea early." She rang a little bell and someone appeared to see what she needed.

***

Rose patted the cushion next to her and Delphi sat.

She's still as unconscious of her elegance and beauty, thought Rose. I wonder if Michael will still see that too, she thought with unease.

"You are well looked after here, it seems," Delphi said.

"Oh yes, it's all amazing. I'm very well looked after. So how old is Flora now? She must be ten, surely. Does she look like you or more like her father? He had such distinctive colouring."

"Yes, she's nearly ten and she has George's eyes but not his red hair. People say she looks like me. She's very pleased to be here and to meet all her family. She'll miss her Australian grandma but I fear she has my adventurous spirit although none of my rebelliousness thank goodness."

Rose noticed how Delphi was avoiding eye contact. She placed her hand on her sister's arm.

"Delphi I'm truly so pleased that you're here," she said and was happier when Delphi's eyes at last met her own.

"You must take Flora to see the school. She will need to attend somewhere. You might consider placing her at Kingshaven and Michael would love to meet her and to see you again too."

Why am I forcing them together? Especially when I can't be there to witness it, Rose thought. I need confirmation that all is over and in the past, I think.

"Oh there's plenty of time for all that." Delphi smiled at her sister. "You're right though. Eventually Flora will have to go to school somewhere. How is it going there?"

"Before all this, things were doing very well. Bedales, Frensham Heights and we at Kingshaven are developing quite a name for being forward thinking and the new face of co-educational education. Our policies are claiming attention in some of the highest places. Having the Duke of Norfolk on the board helps our cause, of course. Wait until you see the place, Delphi. It's magnificent."

"It all sounds fascinating," Delphi said.

"You must visit the chapel. My painting hangs above the altar. It's one of my best works. I've called it 'Not by Might, nor by Power but by my Spirit'." Her voice shone with her enthusiasm."

"That sounds like you dearest," Delphi said.

"It's allegorical, of course."

"That sounds like you too," Delphi said but then wished she hadn't. "I didn't mean to be critical with that remark," she added.

"Please, don't fret. I know I spoke crude words in anger to you once but it's all in the past." Rose picked at her skirt. "The grounds are perfect for outdoor lessons." She changed the subject. "We have a pageant with dance, prose and poetry every year. Parents come for each Speech Day and they have been very complimentary. They've been supportive too during this bout of trouble but it's still a worry for Michael. The bank is always knocking at the door." Her eyes glittered behind her spectacles.

"You mustn't exhaust yourself, Rose, my dear," her Papa said. "All will still be there for you."

"Yes. It's just that I do so miss it all."

"Michael will keep it safe. This new senior mistress seems to be up to it as well. She has embraced the philosophy of the place and I gather the parents like her."

"Michael must miss you," Delphi said. "It won't be long now will it? Before you can leave here, I mean."

"Not long now, Rose," her Papa added.

"I do feel much better." Rose lay back in her chair though and suddenly seemed tired.

"We'll go," he said. "We do not wish to tire you too much."

"Come again soon, Delphi."

"I will." Delphi bent to kiss her sister's forehead, having risen from the seat at Papa's prompting.

"And do go to visit Michael and take Flora to meet him," Rose said again.

Almost as if he had been watching from the wings and right on queue the doctor reappeared.

"Visits little and often are still the best thing. She still gets weary easily." He smiled at Rose and nodded at Delphi. He followed her and Mr Strong as they left the way they had come.

***

At the front door Delphi turned to the doctor. "Thank you," she said.

He smiled at her and his dark eyes made her heart swoop.

"She seems so frail, Dr Harman,"

"It's Doctor Brown," he said.

"Oh yes, I'm so sorry. I was reminded of someone else." She shook her head.

"She's been very, very ill but she's on the mend. A few weeks and she'll be able to go home. We are concentrating now on building up her strength with fresh air and good, nourishing food. We don't want her to succumb to this or anything else while her system is so depleted."

"I think she worries about her husband and the school," Mr Strong said.

"Yes, I think you're correct and that's not good for her either. We try to keep her calm so that she's not fretting. Mind you her husband has had a fright too. When he visited last time, he was very tired when I saw him but he managed to distract her. Will you be visiting him Mrs Dight?"

"I'm sure she will," Mr Strong answered for Delphi while she tried to master her thoughts.

"Yes, yes, I shall and give him my sister's love, of course." Delphi was in such turmoil what with the build-up to the meeting with Rose and the thought of meeting Michael again.

Fancy calling the Doctor by the name of Harman, too. What an idiot! What was I thinking? He reminds me of Rainier though with those dark eyes. That's what I was thinking.

With that, they left and Doctor Brown returned to his patient.

***

He took a stethoscope from his pocket upon his return to Rose. "You mustn't overdo things," he said. "I'm going to listen to your heart."

"Mmm," he said. "It's fine but you must take it easy now. I think this visit has wearied you although from what you told me I imagine it was worry about it before the event as much as the visit itself."

"You're right," Rose admitted. "I've been worrying about it and about my sister visiting my husband." She smiled and shrugged. "I've been here long enough for you to know my entire life history and to know me well, it seems."

"All part of the cure and as we said, ages ago, it's all confidential too. Your sister told me she would give your husband your love. Worrying is not good for you and definitely not part of the treatment."

Rose nodded. It was all very well of Papa to have brought Delphi home. She understood that it was for the best of reasons but she had felt safe and confident with her on the other side of the world. She and Michael had made a good life and although they had no children of their own yet, a source of disappointment to them both, she knew he loved her.

Give him my love, please, dear sister but not your own love, Rose thought.

Chapter 8

The visit to Rose's and Michael's school was organised and Flora was sitting next to Delphi as the car rolled up the long and impressive drive. She would need a place to study for a while anyway, although Delphi was far from sure Michael and Rose would want her at their school. After all, they knew the circumstances of her conception and birth. That was the trouble with returning home. It was fine in Australia. Everyone believed that she had married George and were sympathetic to her for her loss. There was still such a stigma attached to having a child out of wedlock even though it wasn't her fault. Well, not exactly. She regretted none of it and wouldn't have come back at all if her Papa had not persuaded her.

Now, Delphi was pleased to have the excuse and distraction of showing Flora everything when she met Michael for the first time in so many years. How could she forget the fool she had made of herself with him when she was but still a girl? She grew warm at the memory.

The car tyres scattered gravel as they braked outside the front of the building and Delphi stepped out. She put her hand to her hat to hold it in place as she craned her head right back to stare up to the roof line where grey gargoyles glared down at her ominously. Turning to take Flora's hand and glancing across at her Papa, they mounted the long flight of steps towards the heavy front door. By the time they stood before it her legs were aching. Papa pulled the bell handle and they waited.

"It'll be alright," he said sensing her unease as they waited.

She took a deep breath.

They were shown into a large and formal drawing room with settees set at right angles to the great fire place which was laid but not lit. Other chairs were scattered beyond.

"Can I get you anything ma'am, sir?" the housemaid enquired.

They declined and she left with, "The head master won't be long."

Delphi perched on the edge of a seat. She glanced at Flora who was looking around with eyes wide and eyebrows raised. This was so vastly different from what was familiar. Even her Grandpapa Strong's house was not this big. Delphi noted the grand piano with its lid open and music in place. The brocade that cloaked the windows was thick but she saw it was also becoming threadbare although the brass tiebacks were ornate and polished to a high shine. The rug beneath her feet had also seen better days but she could tell it had once been very costly.

Then there were footsteps outside the room on the marble floor and echoing around the great hall through which they had come. The sounds came closer. There was a pause just on the other side of the door. Then the handle turned. The door opened and he was there, framed. Michael.

Delphi had not seen him since before those fateful events of 1917 and she still burned with embarrassment at her foolish proposal to him before that. She remembered her childish infatuation because now she knew it was just that but she also understood the devastation it had caused Rose. Of the deception back then, she was truly ashamed.

He stood before her now, tall and just as handsome although slightly heavier. His blond hair still cascaded across his

55

forehead hiding the scar she was sure must still be there. As he approached she could see streaks of grey that were not evident immediately among the fairness, and lines on his face that had not been there all those years ago.

"Delphi, you are as beautiful as ever." He stretched out his hands to hers. As she took them she marvelled at how the brain can play tricks. She remembered him as he had been and was surprised by the passing of time. He had called her beautiful. Was she still attractive? Rainier had thought so.

But he did not stir her heart as he once had although in all honesty it never was aroused as it had been for her own dear George. For him she had been delirious, mad. She was wise enough to know that back then, before she had met George, with Michael it had been a perverse pleasure she took in upsetting her sister, a power-play that she must have needed to win. Since all that, there had been Rainier, so different with his black hair and flashing dark eyes. Michael's were pale and lifeless compared with those. Oh Lord how her soul cried out silently for him. Her love for Rainier was mature, considered and deep. It was not a flush of youthful infatuation, nor was it cast from desperate times and desires heightened by fear as with George. She tried to imagine him striding between the rows of vines in France, the sun shining upon his head but she couldn't.

Why did she always have to mess up her life and that of others around her? Then if she *had* shared all this history and her subterfuge of Flora's conception Rainier would probably have run a mile anyway. Her own mother had called her a 'dirty girl'. When she had felt the full force of Rose's anger, which was so out of character, it was utterly devastating. She had been a slut and a loose woman but she had never regretted one moment of Flora's being.

She dragged her mind back to the present. As Michael let her go, he turned to Flora. "It's a pleasure to meet you young lady. I can't believe I have a niece of your age. You are very like your mother."

Delphi could see from the look on Flora's face she had heard what Michael said to her when he took her hands upon entering the room and knew her daughter was charmed by him as she had been as a child, with his dimpled cheek, broad grin and his compelling   · stature.

"Would you like to look around the school?" He turned to Mr Strong. "You're welcome to come too, of course, but you're more familiar with things. Shall I ring for tea?"

"I'm fine here, lad. You go. We might have tea when you all return," Mr Strong replied.

The dining room was in the fine tradition of the hunting lodge this place had once been. "What an experience for your students," Delphi said.

The dormitories each held beds for six. "There's a senior in with each group. They have that curtained area at the end," Michael explained. "We're definitely part of the progressive movement so we have a liberal ethos and a relaxed attitude but we also promote responsibility and leadership, reasoning and explanation rather than bossiness and hectoring. That's why we focus upon dance, art and crafts and music too. We're encouraging freedom of thought."

As they emerged into the grounds Flora skipped ahead to look at the fountain and its pond. Delphi watched, her daughter's yellow dress spreading like melted butter as she sat on the low wall. Her trailing fingers created ripples and the sun scattered its bright diamonds around them.

"When we started out, Rose and I were determined to follow John Badley's example at Bedales and ensure co-education here. We want to get away from the unwholesome behaviour and even perversions that can occur in a single sex school. We know co-education is not widely adopted in England because of fear of sex mistakes." He looked sideways at her and stopped walking. He turned to face her. "Delphi I want you to understand that we hold no sense of blame for Flora's birth. Those days of the war were extra-ordinary. George was my dearest friend. He needed your comfort to fulfil his duty."

"Thank you Michael. That means such a great deal to me. She's my world."

"Have you considered schooling for her?"

"Yes but I thought you might not want her here. I can see from what you say I might have misjudged you and your views of me and of her."

"Oh Delphi, I think you have. Rose and I would welcome her and you too should you need a home."

Delphi laughed. "Papa isn't going to want us for ever, I'm sure of that. He has Izzy to look after him and I'm not certain he would want more female clutter these days but we couldn't simply scavenge from you either."

"What if we could come to some sort of business arrangement?"

"What do you mean?" Delphi glanced across at Flora who was still preoccupied with the water.

"We". . ." he hesitated. "You must say if you think it wouldn't work." He looked down at her and seemed awkward.

"I can't give an opinion unless you tell me." She smiled at him, feeling at ease at last.

"We need someone to take control of the kitchens. I don't mean slaving at the stove." He rushed on. "I mean to control the thing, plan the menus, and order the necessary stocks, food and equipment. The senior mistress has been doing it and before that, Rose but it's too much. We need someone with the skills and understanding. It would be small fry for you after what you did in France in the WAACs." He finally paused for breath.

Delphi was taken aback and said nothing while she thought through the possibilities.

"After all, you got an MBE for that. You would be part of the senior team here. It's a critical role not some Cinderella position." He paused again. "Please do consider it. Rose and I talked for simply ages about it. Have I offended you in some way? Please do say something. Rose is as keen as I am. I'm sorry. I have offended you, haven't I? It wasn't meant that way." He looked at his feet and then placed his hand on her arm. "I'm sorry," he said again.

Chapter 9

That night Delphi had so much to think about she couldn't sleep. Tossing about wasn't helping. She grew hot and in her restlessness the covers were getting tangled and wrinkled. Swinging her legs out of bed, she went and stood by the window. The moon was full and cast a glow over the grass to the trees beyond. It was so clear and bright their shadows were long across the lawn and looking up into their branches was a muddled filigree web of darkness.

That's how I feel, she thought; confused and dark. Do I want to set such roots down here? How would I feel living in such close contact with Michael and Rose? How does Rose really feel about that? If only I had heard from Rainier. Clearly it was only a shipboard romance. He would have written if he felt more. How stupid I've been to harbour hopes. Flora needs stability and the school seems to offer that to us both. Papa is being so good but he's used to his routine with Izzy. I would have a purpose if I took over the organisation of the kitchens at the school and Flora would learn and make friends.

She gave an enormous sighed. Why was life always so difficult?

The next morning Delphi was heavy eyed and lack lustre for the day ahead. She must write some letters and then perhaps she and Flora would take a walk and get out from under her Papa's feet. Izzy seemed to need no help either.

Before going downstairs she sat at her little desk and took writing paper. Picking up her pen she wrote to Michael and accepted his offer. Sealing it in the envelope and addressing that she felt slightly better. At least she had made a decision.

"Mummy, I thought you were never coming down." Flora greeted her looking lively and sounding alert. "Grandpa Strong said I shouldn't disturb you, that you were tired but there's so much to go and see."

"Sorry, sweetie, I didn't sleep too well but I'm here now so just let me have a cup of coffee and we'll get started on some adventure, shall we? I have a letter to go and post as well."

"There's a letter here on the plate for you. Who do you think it might be from?"

Delphi's heart gave a leap and then Flora continued. "I don't think it's Granny or Grandad. It's got an English stamp."

Delphi glanced at the letter lying on the salver at the bottom of the stairs. Images of other letters lying there long ago flashed through her mind. She picked this one up with apathy and glanced at the back. No address or indication there.

It's not from Rainier anyway, she thought. That just makes my decision more valid. She felt for the newly written letter in her pocket.

"Have you eaten yet?"

"I had mine ages ago," Flora replied. "Who do think that's from?" She nodded at the envelope in her mother's hand.

"Do me a favour darling and go and ask if I might have coffee then come through to the dining room with me. I'll open it there."

Flora hopped and skipped along with the excitement and anticipation of the young.

Once seated, "Oh, it's from Bea Shearer," Delphi said and started to read. "Ah, she's heard from Rainier. He's getting settled into his new home and sorting out the vineyard and production issues. She speaks of her new grandchild, too."

"Rainier hasn't written to us," Flora said and looked disappointed.

"No, well I'm sure he's far too busy. He'd know that Mrs Shearer would pass along any news, I'm sure."

"Does she say what her grandchild is called? Is it a boy or a girl?"

"You always want to know everything little Miss Sticky Beak." Delphi laughed and tweaked the nose of her off-spring.

"Grandad Dight used to call me that," Flora said.

"When I was young Papa used to call me little Miss Nosey Parker. It means the same thing. Anyway the baby is a boy and he's called John, apparently."

"Can we go and see her and the new baby?"

"I'm sure we could arrange that at some point but not now. Let me get on and then we can go out for a walk. Shall we go into the town and explore there or shall we go across the fields?"

"Oh across the fields definitely," Flora said.

"I'll show you down the lane where my sisters and I used to go when I was young," Delphi said. "There's the little local shop and post office that way. I wonder if the same lady still works there."

As they went, Delphi set Flora the task of collecting something for each letter of the alphabet and she was busy scavenging in the hedgerows for flowers and other things to pop into her little basket. In between exclaiming, praising and helping Delphi had the space to consider the other news in Bea's letter; the news she hadn't shared with her daughter.

"J is such a tricky letter," Flora said, interrupting her mother's thoughts.

"Sorry?"

"Mummy! The letter J. I'm stuck on that on." Flora sounded exasperated.

"Juice. Find a berry of something like that," Delphi suggested.

Flora skipped ahead again, the skirt of her dress bouncing and swinging with the joy of being outside in the country.

So he was asking after us, she thought. Bea referred to '*you both*' though, not to just me. He's probably being polite. I really can't read much into that. I shouldn't anyway. And what if he really did come over to visit as she suggests he said he might. He still doesn't know the truth of Flora's birth.

Her thoughts flowed up and down in similar vein first this way and then that taking her mood on a rollercoaster until Flora interrupted again.

Later, having posted her letter to Michael, she was feeling more positive about their future. She must make another new start and this was as good a way as any. She would prove herself to Rose and all would be well.

When Delphi and Flora returned from their walk a further surprise awaited.

A letter had arrived by the second post while they were out. Delphi didn't recognise this writing either but she recognised the images and the words *poste* and *Republique Francaise* on the stamp. After all she had spent months and months in France herself albeit a long time ago.

She became breathless and her knees wobbled. She felt dizzy. She realised all the longing she had supressed was flinging itself around her head. Flora had run off to find Dora and show her collection basket so Delphi grabbed the letter from the salver on the table and collapsed onto the stairs as her heart bumped in her ears.

Eventually as her shaking subsided she sped up the steps to her room and shutting the door she leaned against it and ripped open the letter. Then she started shaking again. The letter was short but when she reread it straight away she knew she must share everything with Rainier.

My dearest darling Delphi, mon amour, mon coeur,

I have to call you that because it's true, you have my heart and I am incomplete. I miss you. I thought when we said goodbye that would be the end of it but I cannot leave it. I am being swallowed by this great empty hole.

I know there is something you held back from me but I miss you so much I don't care what it is. I don't give a jot. It cannot be so terrible that I would not love you anyway.

My duties here on the estate prevent me from coming to see you immediately but I hope and pray that as soon as I am able you will allow me to visit. You cannot believe how I my life is so bland. Please write to me soon and tell me how you feel. If I am making a fool of myself I shall understand but in my soul I think you miss me too.

I am yours,
Rainier.

Delphi, not prone to tears, staggered to her bed and curled up and cried. She cried for all the lost moments, for her own cowardliness, for all the missed opportunities and her own stupidity in not trusting his good judgement.

Eventually, when she was all cried out, she sat up. Looking in the mirror, she saw her fine slanting eyes were red and they stung. She felt exhausted with emotion. She sat and taking up her brush she passed it through her hair contemplating all that she had read and all that she was feeling. In the end the repetitive motion began to sooth her spirit. She replaced the hairbrush and reaching forwards she took paper and pen from her writing box. This was not going to be easy and it was important to get it right. Against her normal nature to dash through things she sat and thought for a long while before writing the first words.

My dearest Rainier,

I must tell you something and if you detest me after, I shall understand. It concerns Flora and the circumstances of her conception and her birth . . .

Then she screwed it up and threw it in the bin.

Chapter 10

It was the next day before Delphi retrieved the letter she had started but not finished. She would have to tell Rainier some of it so she rewrote the beginning and completed a missive. At the last minute she still she omitted the pertinent fact that she hadn't been married. At the post office she hesitated at the door but taking a deep breath she steeled her resolve and saw the letter on its way.

So beside herself with emotion, it wasn't until later in the day that Delphi considered the other letter that was already winging its way to the school with her acceptance of the job that Michael and Rose offered.

"I really have to go and see Rose first thing in the morning, Papa." Delphi had knocked on her father's study door and was now seated in front of him.

She explained her dilemma.

"From what I understand Rose and Michael would welcome any help you can give. Nothing is certain for you in any other camp, my dear. Take their offer and see what happens. If you want to leave in the future and take up elsewhere then of course you can do that but in the meantime you and Flora will have security, a home and Flora will have an education which will serve her well."

"Thank you for your wise council." Delphi stood and leaned in to kiss her Papa on the cheek. She smelled his tobacco and the roughness of his face transported her back to when she was little more than a child with a whole new life beginning to engulf her.

They had never been demonstrative. Her Papa was from an era when things were not expressed and before she went to Australia life generally, was more formal. That summer, though, had changed her life forever. Rose had shouted her innermost feelings at her and her mama had hardly spoken to her after her initial harsh words on hearing of her condition. She had gone to Australia with George's parents and Flora had been born.

Delphi did go to see Rose but not for a couple of days. If she was going to take the place offered the urgency was diminished. After all, her Papa was correct. There were no promises of anything elsewhere. She needed to be open in her dealings and she craved her sister's respect. They needed to talk, just the two of them so that she could cement her apology for past wrongs and be reassured that all was left behind, genuinely.

Again she headed to conservatory at the sanatorium but this morning the sun had disappeared and the sky was a heavy grey with the real threat of rain.

Perfect, thought Delphi. Huh! Not what this conversation needs.

Then when she arrived there were others present. It wasn't conducive to a private, possibly emotional, conversation.

"There's a small sitting room. Come on, let's go there," Rose said, leading the way.

"You always were the sensitive one," Delphi said and then regretted it when Rose looked back over her shoulder but said nothing. It sounded like a sarcastic criticism and it wasn't meant to be.

Delphi sighed. She seemed to be sighing a lot lately.

"I'm coming home, next week," Rose said. "I shall have to be careful but I'm fretting about my absence. Doctor Brown had a long conversation with us and has finally agreed to let me go." She closed the door behind them and went to sit down in the little room.

They chatted inconsequentially for several minutes. Neither was willing to commit, it seemed.

"So, Michael has put to you our proposition and he tells me you have accepted." There seemed to be some coolness about her sister and Delphi was overcome with misgivings all over again.

"Look, Rose, if you think it would cause problems, me being there . . ."

"No, we discussed it at length. It seems the perfect solution for all of us."

"I'm not sure how long I would be there. I met someone."

"Oh . . .?" Rose's voice ascended in a question and for the first time Delphi saw the glimmer of a smile.

She shared all that had happened between her and Rainier. She told Rose about her letter to him explaining some of what happened with George all those years ago and that Flora was the result of an out-door liaison which probably to him would seem wanton.

"I must explain to you, too, Rose. The lies I told you about Michael . . ."

"Hush, Delphi. We were children."

"But . . ."

"I know, but it worked out in the end. Michael and I are very happy. I do believe he has loved me well. We all grew up. The war changed everything."

"It did. I loved George to the exclusion of all else. Now I've met Rainier. I don't know what will happen there. Maybe nothing. But working with you and Michael will be a wonderful opportunity for me and especially for Flora. Yet again, I owe you much."

"No you don't. You're my sister and we will gain as much if not more from having you there taking a great weight from our shoulders." Rose stood. "Come here,"

Delphi moved towards her sister and they enfolded each other. Rose felt like air, so tiny and thin was she. Tears came to Delphi and despite the fact that she raised her eyes to the ceiling to prevent a tell-tale cascade, the moisture slid down her cheeks.

"We will be a good team," Rose said as she stood back and the smile this time reached her eyes.

***

The following week was madness. Delphi visited the school again and tried to familiarise herself with all that she would need to do to take on such a responsibility as was asked of her. She wrote copious notes and made lists until her fingers ached. It was true, as Michael had intimated. Whilst it was a big task it did not match up to the size of her responsibilities in France when feeding hundreds of troops and never being sure of things was far more complex.

The little flat that she and Flora had been given was fine for their needs but it still needed a thorough spring clean and Delphi wanted to rearrange the furniture to make it more like her own home. Flora would sleep in the dorm with others of her age but she would come here at the weekends when many of the others also went home.

After having spoken to Rose, she planned to take Flora up to Manchester on the train to buy uniform, too.

"We have tried to build a good reputation and so the best up-market establishment must be associated with Kingshaven. It caused a little uproar in the family when Michael announced to his father that we had commissioned Kendal, Milne and Faulkner instead of the family firm. The one we have chosen is known as the Harrods of the North, though. That's the level at which we are beginning to operate." Rose spoke with pride.

"It must certainly have helped having the Duke's patronage even though he no longer owns the premises as such," Delphi said. "It's a magnificent building. You have come far, Rose."

Her sister laughed. "We certainly have when I think how Michael started in the garage at the cottage with no more than five children from the village."

Until they moved into the school, every day Delphi looked at the salver at the bottom of the stairs despite her resolve not to. Her eyes strayed each morning she descended and each morning she felt crushing disappointment. While there was no letter from Rainier she imagined the disgust he must be feeling at her revelations to him.

She immersed herself in her new work. Dressed in a white smothering overall and with her new neat bobbed hair covered, she busied herself for long hours. Her staff needed some further training to match her exacting standards and menus needed updating.

"I think I might write a book," she said to Rose one day. "A cookery book but one which will also be a training manual for young people. What do you think?"

"Are we not keeping you busy enough?"

"You are. It's just a vague thought at the moment." She smiled at her sister. "How do think Flora is doing? It's all very different for her. I've tried to keep out of it as much as possible and let her find her own feet. She doesn't say much."

"So many parents say the same thing when they ask their youngsters what they have done. Children seem to find it hard work to recount everything. I've been keeping a special eye on her. How could I not? She's beginning to settle."

"She has talked a lot about Edith. They seem to be making friends."

"Edith hasn't been here long either so it's a friendship of convenience but, I don't know, I think they may become really good friends. They complement each other."

***

Flora joined her mother at the breakfast table. It was small and tucked into the bay window but overlooked the front drive and the fountain. The sun beamed in and the room was light and fresh since Delphi had smiled at the handyman and got him to add a fresh coat of paint above the dado rail and across the ceiling.

Ever open in her dealings Flora said, "I like it here. My English family are very kind. I do miss Granny Dight of course." Delphi knew she had added this last phrase because she thought she ought to. Flora was always kind and very considerate, even at her tender age. "We had dance outside yesterday. Miss Healey told Edith and I we did very well. There's going to be a pageant. Everyone's going to be in it. I don't think we'll get top parts like the speaking parts or anything because we're so new but I don't mind. It sounds like great fun. Frightfully *mezzo-brow*, one of the seniors said."

Delphi smiled at her enthusiasm.

"I don't even know what that means but it will be ever so good," Flora continued. "Miss Healey said we would move through the ages from the Stone Age to The Gifts of Science. There'll be dressing up and dancing and poetry. We started to learn figure marching. We really had to think hard. It was quite tricky. Edith said . . . ," and on she flowed.

Delphi listened and nodded and added a comment here and there.

"Aunt Rose said . . . Can I call her that? When I'm in school I say Mrs Redfern."

Delphi nodded.

"Aunt Rose is lovely and kind. She always smiles and when Joseph was foolish and unkind to Peter Moore she said we had to understand why he did that and not just be cross with him. We don't see Uncle Michael so much but everyone likes him. He takes us for worship each morning of course. He's much funnier than when we went to the services on the ship. When we sing in the chapel it echoes all around and sounds lovely. Mummy did you hear me?"

"Sorry darling, I was miles away but only for that bit."

"What were you thinking about?"

"I was remembering things we did on the SS Jervis Bay. You said 'on the ship' and it set me remembering."

"We haven't heard from Rainier, have we? I hoped we might," Flora said in her innocence.

"Mmm, me too," Delphi said. "Right, we have the whole day. What would you like to do?" She stood and began to busy herself clearing the table so Flora got up to help.

The next day a letter awaited Delphi when she returned to her flat.

Chapter 11

Dear Delphi and Flora too, (of course),

I hope this finds you well and happy. Your last letter was full of news and it was lovely to hear how Flora is settling into her new school. You sound very busy yourself with so much to organise.

My grandson is growing quickly and Sophie, my daughter, takes him out in his pram every day for the fresh air. I often go too and, in fact, am sitting on a bench in the shade of a tree in the park to write this to you while they continue on a circuit.

Now, the reason I'm writing is a delicate one. I was sworn to secrecy but as I haven't yet responded to that I think it would be alright to bend the rules a little. The thing is, a mutual friend from the good ship Jervis Bay is thinking of visiting me. I suspect that is a ploy and that this person will visit elsewhere in England whilst here.

There, really I have told you nothing have I? I thought you might like to know and be a little prepared. I'm not sure when this will be.

The person in question is particularly busy at the moment. On the farm place there are many workers who need to get back into good habits and the crop itself needed much trimming and improvement in many ways, I hear. It seems at this time of year the vines grow rapidly and unwanted shoots must be kept to a minimum or the fruit will not flourish. Whoops. I've said too much.

Ah, John needs changing apparently and Sophie says we must go. I'll finish this and get it off to you, my dear. If I hear more news of our friend I shall be sure to let you know as soon as I can.

Best wishes to you both.
Your good friend,
Bea

The letter had been forwarded to Delphi at the school by Izzy as had any other letters that had arrived, although they were few and certainly nothing from Rainier.

Delphi plonked herself down on a chair and re-read it. She wouldn't say anything to Flora about this, not yet. It may come to nothing, anyway. A hundred questions buzzed around her brain. Why had he not written to her? Was he just going to see Bea and avoid her? She wouldn't blame him for that. Why would he come all that way to see an old lady and not come to see her, though? Again she wondered by he hadn't been in contact with her. She thought the worst. He won't come here. I better get on and forget all this nonsense.

She stuffed the letter in her pocket and decided to burn it when the fire was lit this evening. No need to upset Flora with news of something that wasn't going to happen. Right, where was the order pad for the grocer?

***

Flora and Edith had just emerged from their English class clutching school copies of Charles
Kingsley's '*The Water Babies*'.

"Let's head down the bank to the oak tree," Edith said. "I really want to know what Tom thinks when he sees himself all grubby in Ellie's mirror."

"Me too," Flora said. "Do you think they'll fall in love?"

"It's not really that kind of story, I don't think. Anyway Miss Pryce wouldn't let us read that sort of book. Too racy for her." They giggled as they ran.

Flopping down on the feeble course grass beneath the ancient tree, Flora said, "We've only got about half an hour. It's a bit spiky here anyway." She brushed the twigs and old acorns from under her to make a more comfy spot."

Then she said, "I'd really like to read 'The Thirty-Nine Steps'. It's by someone called John Buchan. My mother was reading it. It's about spies in Scotland. She said it was really exciting. I'd like to be a spy."

"Oh yes, me too," Edith agreed. Do you know what a spy does?"

"Not really but it sounds daring." She opened her book to get onto safer territory.

A short while passed and Edith leaped up. "I can hear voices. It must be the seniors coming out. We'll be late and get a right wigging. Come on."

They ran for it at full tilt across the field and arrived panting just as the last of the class were walking into their next lesson.

"You look a bit hot, girls. I hope you haven't been running around school," the teacher said.

"Oh no, Miss," said Flora.

"It's Miss Pryce, Flora."

"Sorry, Miss Pryce." Flora glanced at Edith and grinned. "I'd love to spy on her," she whispered as they took their seats. That would be a tale to tell. I'm sure she has a secret life and she's not as prim as she makes out."

"You have something to add to the conversation, Flora?"

"No, Miss Pryce."

***

"I think Flora's becoming more confident," Rose said. Delphi entered the salon after tea was finished and she had set the two kitchen maids on clearing up and washing the dishes.

"Oh?" Delphi sat down opposite her sister.

"Don't frown," Rose said. "It's a minor matter but I thought you'd like to know. She was caught passing notes in class and when the teacher asked her to read it out she flatly refused. I think she was playing to the audience a little so she has been awarded a detention."

"Oh dear," Delphi said. "Sorry. That doesn't seem like her. She can be bold but not usually rude."

"She wasn't rude at all. She refused to hand over the paper with extreme politeness. Actually just between us, I think the teacher asked for it."

"Who was it?"

"Miss Pryce but please don't say anything to her. I've had a word with her about how she might have handled it differently."

"I'll have words with Flora. I think you're right though. She's finding her feet as you say, and gaining independence that she's not had before."

"A different kind, I imagine," Rose said.

"You're right. She used to roam for miles and ride on her own around the station but she always had the security of the family each evening and the hired hands would often see her around when they were out seeing to the sheep. Crikey, I hope she's not going off the rails."

"You sounded so Australian when you said that." Rose laughed. "She'll be fine. In my experience and I have seen it many times, children will try out behaviours but they almost always revert to form and follow family values."

"I hope so. I'll speak to her anyway," Delphi said.

***

Delphi settled into her new role with ease. Menus and ordering was simple for the numbers concerned and her book-keeping skills resurfaced with comparative ease. She liked the staff, she saw little of Michael but when she did, things were easy between them and Rose was affectionate and natural. Flora continued to be lively and from time to time she over-stepped the mark a little but nothing too bad.

Then she had a visitor.

Mindful almost constantly of Bea's last letter. She ripped of her white cap and overall and running her hands through her hair as she hurried along the corridor she wondered who it could be, hoping above all it might be Rainier but not daring to believe. Arriving in the great hall, by the front door stood her youngest sister, Izzy. Her heart plummeted. Not the one who she wished to see particularly, although pleasant enough. Delphi had not seen much of her after returning from Australia and moving here so she was a little puzzled that she had come calling.

"Hello, little sister," Delphi said, rallying her spirits and moving to kiss the arrival. "This is a lovely surprise. We don't often see you here, I believe. Is Papa alright? There aren't any problems are there?"

"No, no, nothing like that," Izzy said as she removed her coat but keeping on her hat.

"Put it on the chair there." Delphi pointed.

"I wasn't exactly passing but I had a meeting of my ladies German group. We were discussing the rise of this man Hitler and how he says that Germany is steadily slipping towards communism because of the economic problems like bankruptcies and higher unemployment. People over there are borrowing more and more. It's a bit worrying."

"I was reading something about it the other day," Delphi said. "You always were interested in the country, even as a girl."

"More so since I've lived there. Papa wanted me home because Mama died and you were coming and . . . It's complicated."

Delphi knew they had never been close. Was Izzy resentful and blaming her for having to give up her German friends? Had she returned to England because she, Delphi, had been asked by Papa to come back?"

"Would you go again?"

"Like a shot. I've lots of friends there."

"So what brings you to see me here today?"

Delphi was uncomfortable and sought the mundane. Had she really affected so many people's lives with that reckless act so long ago and was it still reaching out to those around her as much as herself?

"There was a telephone call for you. I took it and said I would pass the message along."

"Oh?" Was Izzy being deliberately awkward by imparting the information so slowly?

"Yes, the line was very crackly but we managed to hold a brief conversation."

She paused.

"And? Who was it? Izzy get on with it."

"This fellow Rainier that you seem to have set your cap at."

Chapter 12

"Izzy for goodness sake tell me all and I haven't 'set my cap' as you say. We met, we were friends, that's all. So what was the message?"

"He wanted to know if he could speak to you so I told him you were no longer living there."

"So what did he say to that?" This was so frustrating of Izzy.

I gave him the number and the address of the school. He asked me to tell you he had rung. That's it."

"That's all? Did he say where he was ringing from?"

"No."

"Didn't he say anything else at all?" Delphi was becoming increasingly annoyed with her sister.

"No that was it."

"You could have asked him," Delphi said.

"Delphi! It wasn't for me to ferret out information. Now if you want to thank me for making this special trip to inform you then please do. You can be so grumpy and ungrateful still. After that I'll go and see Rose."

"Oh Izzy, I'm sorry." Delphi breathed out her tension and was contrite. She and Izzy had never got along as children. That was why Rose had to share bedrooms with their youngest sibling and Delphi had one of her own. "It was very kind of you. I don't deserve you. I'm just tense about the whole thing. Come along, let's go together to find Rose and I'll arrange some tea for all of us."

She linked her arm through that of her sister and they went in search of the one who had always been the peacekeeper.

***

Delphi's mind was everywhere but on her work over the next week. Luckily it was all so easy that it didn't take much concentration and the kitchen staff were beginning to function at a higher level and to think for themselves. The ordering of supplies was her responsibility alone however. Fortunately the grocer was perceptive and when he received an order for a hundred times one hundredweight sacks of potatoes instead of ten, he rang the school and asked for clarification.

Rose followed up the telephone call by searching out Delphi in her little office off the kitchen.

"Is everything alright? I looked around the kitchen as I came through but it was only a glance. Everything seems as neat and orderly as it should be but you seem distracted, dearest.

"Yes, fine. Why do you ask?" Delphi felt a frisson of worry. "Have I done something wrong?"

Rose explained the telephone call. "It seems so unlike you not to double check. Is this business with Flora worrying you?"

Yet again Flora had been in trouble only this time it had been more serious.

"To be honest, Rose, it's that and the information that came from Izzy about Rainier telephoning. I just don't know where I stand. I had set my mind to never seeing him again. It was just a fleeting friendship. I never divulged the real issue of Flora's father. It was my sin and mine to live with. That telephone message set it all off again but there has been nothing since and now this business with Flora is upsetting and disturbing. I'm not sure how to handle that. If I make too much she'll start to resent me but I can't ignore it. She's never been a difficult child who causes me to worry so."

"The worst thing for children is to be ignored. Maybe she feels your distance and turmoil. I know we don't want to give credence to silly behaviour by making too much of it but on this occasion her safety was a stake. She and I spoke as I told you but maybe she's craving your attention. It's the first time she's not had it all now she's not living with you in the same way. She's lost the attention of grandparents too."

"You're right. It's all my fault."

"That's not what I meant at all. It's no-one's fault. It's the way things have developed and she has to come to terms with the changes. You can't keep her that close forever."

"I'll speak to her tomorrow when she comes home to our flat," Delphi said.

Something else to worry about, she thought, after she told Rose she would contact the grocer about the correction.

Having grovelled down the telephone she made herself a cup of tea and went to sit in her office where she planned what to say to the recalcitrant Flora.

***

"I'm not going to be cross with you. I know you've already spoken about it with Aunt Rose." Delphi was determined to be reasonable and understanding. That was the way she had planned it the day before. "I just need to understand. Why on earth were you on the roof in the middle of the night?" She was aware that her voice was already rising.

"I had a wager with the other girls in the dorm."

"A wager? What about?"

"We were talking about spies, like in your book. You know, the Thirty-Nine Steps. It sounds such a good book. I do wish you'd let me read it."

"You're deviating, Flora." Delphi made her voice sound firm.

"Miss Pryce has been such a dragon."

"You're not making any sense. That doesn't explain why you were doing such a mad-cap, stupid thing."

"You said you weren't going to be cross," Flora reminded her and tears looked in danger of appearing.

"No." Delphi took a huge intake of breath. "No, you're right. Carry on. What was the wager?"

"I was saying I wanted to be a spy when I grow up. It was private conversation with Edith but one of the other girls was listening in and started making fun. We had a bit of an argument. She told me I was childish and stupid and knew nothing about spying so I told her I did."

Flora hung her head.

"And do you?" Delphi was tempted to smile but managed to hold it in.

"Not really but I told her I did and that I could prove it. I know it was bragging but she was being so annoying."

"So what happened then?"

"She said I couldn't even find out what colour nightie Miss Pryce wears."

"What? You risked everything to find that out? I don't believe it. This is ridiculous." All sense of Delphi's restraint and mirth vanished. "I can't believe you would be so stupid. How did you get up onto the roof anyway? And what were you going to do from there? All I can say is it's just as well the caretaker heard you and shone his torch up. For goodness sake, Flora."

"Don't shout at me," she wailed.

"How did you get up there? I think I need to know that at least." Delphi pressed her daughter for answers.

There's a window in the attic and the catch has stuck so it doesn't close properly. I climbed out onto the roof and scrambled along to the parapet and jumped down onto the flat bit above the teachers' wing."

"You could have been killed, you foolish child. At the very least you could have injured yourself badly." Then she had another thought. "You could have knocked slates off and they might have landed on Mr Swift's head while he did his rounds and killed him instead."

Flora looked horrified. "I didn't think." The tears started to fall.

"Oh Flora!"

"I'll never live this down. They'll all know I failed and they'll laugh at me even more. I already get teased because I sound different and I don't have a father."

"I beg your pardon?" Delphi had the force taken from her voice. "What did you say? You don't have a father? You do, darling child. You do. He was killed fighting for what he believed, fighting for this country, miles from his own home."

Delphi started shaking and her own eyes stung at what Flora had said as well as the thought she could have lost her too.

"Come here."

She enfolded her child and they both wept and their heavy tears were like cement, binding them together.

"Tell Aunt Rose if you are being teased. Tell me and I'll give them extra lumpy mashed potatoes." They both laughed. "Don't hold anything back from me. We'll sort it out together."

"I'll manage it," Flora said between post crying gulps. "If I can't be a spy, perhaps I'll be like Mary in '*The Secret Garden*'. Well, not rude like she is at the beginning but I'll discover a secret hiding place and meet a sad boy and make him better."

"You have too much imagination. I hesitate to say you read too much but . . ." Delphi tweaked Flora's nose.

"Shall we go outside for a while and get some fresh air? Let's wash our faces and get straightened up."

Flora nodded.

Having donned cardigans against the cool breeze, Flora, no longer quite so subdued, ran ahead down the stairs. Delphi could hear voices as she began to descend.

Someone to have a look around, perhaps a prospective parent, she thought.

Being in front, Flora saw who it was before Delphi. She suddenly let out a great shout.

"Mummy come and see who's here. Come quickly."

Chapter 13

Rainier stood in the hall, looking awkward, with his hat twirling round and round in his hands. Delphi stood stock still halfway down the stairs taking in the sight of his dark hair and broad-shouldered physique. She could think of nothing to say for several moments. As he heard her descent he took a step forward and then stopped, looking up at her. Then Flora flung herself at him forcing him to take his eyes from Delphi and to gaze at the top of her daughter's shining dark hair as the youngster put her arms around his waist. Although now eleven, she did not have the inhibitions of a child brought up in England and saw nothing wrong in greeting a dear friend thus even though it was months since they had seen each other. He tousled her head.

"Hello, bright young thing," he said.

Delphi was hampered by her sudden self-conscious shyness.

Just then Rose came through from the kitchens. "Ah there you are," she said. "I was looking for you. This gentleman has come a long way to see you, I believe, and Flora I was looking for you too. I really need your help with my wool winding, if you wouldn't mind."

"Aunt Rose, I'd really rather talk with Rainier."

"I know, my dear but if you help me now, when Mr Harman and your mummy are ready perhaps they would have tea in our sitting room and you could come too instead of eating in the student's dining room. We have Madeira cake so it would be a special treat and you will be such a great help to me."

With the bribery and attention, Flora went happily enough with her aunt and Delphi descended the rest of the stairs and went to greet Rainier, having had some moments to collect herself.

As he held out both his hands she had little option but to take them. He leaned towards her and kissed her, first on her left cheek and then on her right. She took a breath and smelled the familiar scent of lemons as his roughened cheek brushed hers. She was transported back to the ship and their time together. Her knees trembled and there was a quiver deep within her lower middle.

"I've missed you so," he said, his accented English arousing complex emotions in Delphi.

She'd missed him too. She knew that but there were issues in her past about which he was only half aware from her letter. What would he say when he heard all the detail? Perhaps she need not divulge her secrets after all. She experienced moments of indecision. She could continue to pretend that Flora's father had died after they were married. Surely he need never know the truth and her shame of the act committed out of wedlock. She had to think of Flora too, didn't she? She didn't want her forever tainted in his eyes. Social distinction of such things was abhorred and women were shunned as evil. Living in Australia had been so far away and the lie she and George's parents had used so often almost became fact; almost but not quite. She knew the truth and so did her sister, Rose, and Michael. What sort of a life would she have based upon untruths and deception?

"Why are you frowning? I'd hoped you'd be pleased to see me," he said and rubbed his thumb across her forehead to erase the lines that had formed. "Now I'm wondering if I have misremembered and misread our feelings."

"No, no you haven't but . . . but there are things I must tell you and after that you may wish to leave and I shall understand." Delphi pulled her shawl across her and folded her arms, slightly hunching forwards in protective stance.

"Oh Delphi, my dearest, I have wondered for so long what could be so terrible that you cannot share it with me. I knew back on the ship that there was a barrier between us and yet I was also sure you had feelings for me."

Delphi looked over her shoulder, aware that they stood in the large hallway from which doors and corridors led away. There could be prying eyes and flapping ears to their conversation.

"Let's go outside and walk and I shall try hard to be open and honest," she said.

She led them across the lawns towards the trees. There was always peace and security among their tall green, grey trunks. They must have seen many things and shared many secrets, these great ancient beech trees. The golden bed of leaves discarded by the branches in early spring when the new fresh green shoots pushed them off the twigs lay beneath their feet crunching and swishing as they walked and the cups of jettisoned nuts cracked. This wood was so different to the one about which she was about to speak. There, the rhododendron bushes and carpet of bluebells was such a blessed relief for George from the mud and the blood and the horror.

"He was so frightened to go back and face what must be endured. Yet he knew he must. That was true bravery, knowing what lay ahead."

"I understand all that," Rainier said in a quiet undertone.

"Of course, you do. You were in just that position on another front," Delphi said.

"So I am in the right place to understand how it was for him and I can guess how difficult it was for you, too."

"He needed something to take with him. I wanted to give him a memory full of cleanliness and love. We loved each other in the fullest sense and completely. Afterwards he told me we would marry as soon as possible and I believe he meant it. It was said after, not before. It was no false promise. Flora was the result, although he never knew that. He died at Flers and was buried there. Later his grave must have been blown apart as the front moved back and forth and the bombardments were ruthless because he was never found. This great new memorial they are starting to build in France, the one designed by Sir Edwin Lutyens, they say his name will be there as one of the missing."

Rainier was silent. He was silent for what, to Delphi, seemed a long time. She glanced up sideways briefly to observe his features and try to gauge his emotions about her revelation. She was tempted to gabble on to fill the emptiness but managed to refrain. This was a shock to him, she could tell. She stopped walking and turned to leave him. That was it. She had been honest and open which was necessary if they were to proceed with any kind of trusting relationship but if it was too much for him, she understood. What she had done was dirty. Her mother had said that. Her sister had screamed abuse at her which was uncharacteristic of Rose, although to be fair that was more about the lies she had told Rose regarding Michael. She had been a selfish youth she thought as she walked away. Dirty and selfish. No way could he want her.

"It's to be the largest Commonwealth Memorial to the Missing in the world," he said to her retreating figure.

She stopped but did not turn because tears were streaming down her lovely face.

"Perhaps we will go there one day, together, and find his name and lay some flowers in his memory," he continued.

At that she turned. Her shawl fell to the ground as she ran to him. His arms enfolded her and she sobbed into his shoulder, all her pent-up fear and dread slowly washing away as she wept.

"I've been so frightened . . . of how you would feel . . . about Flora, never mind despising . . . me for what . . . I did." Loud gulping sobs punctuated her words.

"People who were not there will not understand. They were dreadful, horrific times and people behave differently when under such extreme pressure. What you did, you did for the most caring of reasons and if things had been different we would not have met. How could I not be grateful for your history, every moment of it?"

Delphi looked up at Rainier then and saw tears in his eyes too. He chuckled and she recognised his self-consciousness.

"What a pair we are," he said wiping his eyes with the back of his hand whilst still holding her with the other. "I imagined all kinds of things but I didn't guess this. There are many worse things that people do. Your actions do not count among them."

With that he tilted her chin and brought his mouth to hers in a long and gentle kiss.

"Come along," he said. "We better go back for that tea and cake."

"So you are not disgusted by me? You won't assume I shall lie here in these woods for you?"

"Oh Delphi, do you think so little of me?"

"No, I don't. In reality I don't. I'm sorry."

"Come here." He drew her to him again and silenced her with more kisses which were eager and hard. "We really had better go back, now," he said. "Maybe we will tell them we are to be married, if you will have me, that is. I'm a poor wretch with an ancient French vineyard in the middle of nowhere and I work long hours but I want to marry you Delphi Dight. Will you come to me in France? Will Flora be happy to have me as her second-best Papa?"

"She never knew her first but you better ask her yourself. As for me I should love to be Madame Harman. I love you Rainier."

She had said those words, finally. She knew George would be happy for her and so she was at peace at last.

If you enjoyed this, the story continues in *Flora's War*, a full length novel coming soon and continuing the saga of the Strong Sisters. The prologue and first chapter follow.

Flora's War
Prologue

Spring 1932

The first time they went to Thorelière Flora was little more than a child at fifteen.

"It smells lovely," she'd said. "I think it must be all the little flowers along the banks. I remember all the French names you taught me, Rainier, when we first came to live over here with you."

"The years are speeding by. Mmm, you thought the spring cinquefoil was a French name and yet we call it . . .."

She interrupted her step-father, *"Fleurs de potentille de printemps."* She laughed. "What a mouthful for such a tiny little yellow flower."

As they'd turned the bend in the lane, there was the house. Rainier had stopped the horse and she was aware of the glance he gave Delphi across the top of her head. Flora's mouth dropped open as she took in all before them.

The house was tall and grey with terracotta tiles and shutters of blue that had paled in the strong sunlight. The blooms of wisteria hung in drooping fulsomeness lending a soft lushness to the property.

Arriving in the courtyard the family had come out to greet them. Jean shook hands with his brother, Rainier, and introduced his wife, Francine, to Delphi and Flora. She kissed them and welcomed them. Then he put his hand on his son's shoulder.

"This is Luca," he said. "He must be about your age, Flora." He gave him a gentle shove and the tall gangly lad stepped forward to kiss her on each cheek.

"Don't think you're going to worm your way in here," he hissed in her ear before moving back to greet the adults.

She regarded him coolly but somewhere deep in her young subconscious she knew this place was to be of immense importance to her.

Chapter 1

June 1940

"Flora, in the name of . . . whatever, hurry up. You haven't got time to do all this. They'll be here. You were there when Marcelle telephoned and that was quarter of an hour ago. I told you, they're coming." Delphi was aware of her voice rising in panic.

"I'm going to get the car out," Rainier shouted from below.

"What are you doing? Come. Now." Delphi turned to leave.

"I just . . ."

"No!"

Flora was now a woman herself at nearly twenty-three, certainly no longer an infant but always her child. Delphi knew she shouldn't be chiding her so but it was the worry making her snappy, like a snake churning its way through her stomach.

She heard the crunch of tyres on the gravel outside the window and heaved the scratched old leather suitcase into which she had rapidly flung some things. God only knew if she'd grabbed what was appropriate."

She struggled down the steps from the *porte d'entrée* onto the driveway.

No moon she thought, glancing up. At least something is on our side.

Her heart pounded in her ears. She felt breathless and a bit sick. The weight of her world and her suitcase was awkward on the steps in this hell-black night. An image flashed into her mind of the ship's gangplank and how different carrying this bulk had been back then, twelve years ago. Glorious, exciting, sun-singing years, they were. And now this. Pétain, the Lion of France, feathering his nest and cosying up to the Nazis when he'd fought Germany so valiantly the last time. The last time, oh hell! That was the war to end them all and it had been hell.

Was it because she was still English at heart that she felt differently to many of her local French friends about this new Free Zone?

She listened. Silence. No sound of vehicles yet. No tank tracks rolling. It won't be long though, she thought.

"Flora, please . . ."

Her daughter pounded down the steps behind her with a bag stuffed to over-flowing. Rainier came round the corner of the house to meet them. He took the case from Delphi without a word. She couldn't see but imagined his beloved face grim and sad to be leaving his family home. Who would tend the vines now? Who would remember to trim the shoots and who would be bothered anyway? The estate workers might continue in a half-hearted way but there would be no-one to chivvy them along and no-one with whom to celebrate another successful year in the autumn.

Tears stung her eyes as she ran back to get coats from the cupboard. She grabbed a headscarf that she had carelessly flung down only yesterday. That would have to do. They couldn't waste more time. Oh there was so much that she was leaving; so many memories and treasures.

"Delphi, sit in there." Rainier indicated the driver's seat. "Flora, we must push it to the end of the drive. We can't risk Pierre or any of the other workers hearing us leave. It's for their safety as well as ours."

Delphi was aware that getting the car rolling was hard and her added weight wasn't helping, she was sure. Once it was going she steered as best she could in the dark. She wound the window down the easier to see the grass verge and she strained to listen for the approach of the enemy she knew was coming. It was hard to hear above the noise they made despite trying to be so quiet. Every turn of the tyres, every footstep seemed to echo. If they didn't get away now they would never get into the new *Zone Libre* and living under occupation was not in Rainier's psyche. At least they had talked and talked about this, late into many nights, in the event of France falling but they never expected it to happen so soon, so quickly.

They were to travel to the house of his nephew at Thorelière just south of the river Cher and not far from the chateau of Chenonceau. It was just inside the Free Zone and not too distant from their home here. Rainier had spent time there in his youth and the family had visited many times so they knew many local people and Rainier was respected as an adult. Delphi knew how desperately sad all this was for him. The childhood gems of experience ingrained in his soul, memories of his long-gone parents and a brother killed serving his country but to whom he had been close as they grew up, hiding amongst the vines and scaling rocks and streams here in his ancestral home.

She gulped a sharp intake of breath. What was that? She was sure she heard a distant rumbling with the sound of metal on metal screeching across the once peaceful countryside.

No. Oh no. Hurry. We must hurry. What if we are caught like this? In the dark. In the middle of the night. It's so obvious we are running away.

"Should I start it? I can hear them, I'm sure." She forced a loud whisper although she wanted to shout. She wanted to scream, go away!

"We mustn't lose our cool. We have a short time." Rainier puffed. His lungs, never good since Ypres were struggling with the extra exertion.

"Rainier, I'm scared," Delphi heard Flora whisper.

"It's alright *ma petite*. We'll be fine. Not much further and we'll be far enough away from the cottages."

Delphi had never felt so frightened, usually so brave and fearless, reckless even in her youth. She remembered utter soul-wrenching sadness when George, Flora's father, had been killed on the Somme not even knowing about his offspring and not having had time to marry her. She knew the exhilarating disquiet of uncharted experiences when she travelled all the way to Australia with his parents to have his child. This was different. This was desperate stomach-churning terror of a known enemy. What if they didn't make it in time? What if they were caught before reaching comparative safety? Would they be shot or worse for Flora? She'd heard such awful stories recently.

In her youth, Delphi would not have been so fearful.

Perhaps it's because I have a child. I have a full and happy life here, or I have had. I don't want to lose it. I don't want this change. I'm happy again as we are. She felt a new wave of dread and panic flow through her, heightening her senses and churning her stomach. Blood pounded in her ears or was that the thunder of lorries and other military vehicles.

"Surely we can start it now," Delphi said with her head out of the window. "We have to get going. They'll be coming down the hill soon."

Rainier and Flora stopped pushing. Delphi opened the driver's door and twisted in the seat to leap out so that her husband could get behind the wheel.

"Look," she nodded at the tree- line.

There was a definite illumination which was confidently waving up into the sky.

"How dare they shine their lights so arrogantly? Aren't there aeroplanes from the allies to be afraid of?" Delphi asked.

"Evidently not," Rainier answered. "Come, my love, let's go." Without looking back at the solid shades of the house he climbed into the driver's seat.

Delphi held the door as Flora collapsed into the back and pushing it shut as quietly as she could she ducked her head in a shudder as it closed with what seemed a deafening bang. No lights appeared at any cottage windows and she took her place next to her husband as he started the engine.

"I'm not putting the lights on. We'll have to go slowly and hope for the best," Rainier said as he turned the handle to wind up the window.

The noise of the engine, as they left the estate behind, seemed dangerously loud. As they snaked their way up the hill and left the village and all they loved, Delphi realised her shoulders were tensed against all that lay ahead as well as behind. She took a deep breath and made herself relax them for Flora's sake and so that she could concentrate on the road for Rainier.

Near the top of the hill, just before they descended to the start of the next, Rainier pulled over and turned his head back. Delphi looked back too. There was the outline of several buildings, some long and low, others squat and square among the floss of trees. The church steeple in the centre of the village was easily discernible and familiar pointing up to the heavens like a sword, even though the sky was so dark and moonless. As they watched in silence he took her hand and raised it to his lips. Headlights appeared around a distant corner and began to crawl down the road; an evil alien insect with tentacles proliferating across all it passed.

Delphi covered Rainier's hand with hers and they turned back to face the route ahead.

He will not be content to sit it out in his uncle's house, I know he won't, she thought with dread. Flora has been at peace here, too. Rainier has given her a secure and safe home after her years of being at war with herself. What will life hold for her now?